THE SURGEON

A Curvy Girl MC Romance

Nichole Rose

CONTENTS

Dedication   V

About the Book   1

1. Prologue   3

2. Chapter One   8

3. Chapter Two   19

4. Chapter Three   31

5. Chapter Four   45

6. Chapter Five   63

7. Chapter Six   85

8. Chapter Seven   98

9. Chapter Eight   112

10. Chapter Nine   125

11. Epilogue   134

Author's Note   143

Silver Spoon MC   144

Instalove Book Club   146

The Heir   147

Crash Into You   149

Follow Nichole   151

More By Nichole Rose   153

About Nichole Rose   157

DEDICATION

To my partner-in-crime, Loni Ree. BG and I are so excited to be on this adventure with you and Beau! We adore you!

About the Book

An MC murdered her sister. To save her niece, this curvy girl's only choice is to place her trust and heart into the hands of another.

Tate Grimes
When people hear biker, they assume trouble.
That's not me or my MC.
I'm a respected pediatric surgeon.
I just happen to like the road at my back, the wind in my face, and the MC brotherhood.
My job and the MC are all I want...
Until Samara Lansing blows into my life and changes everything.

She's a fierce warrior determined to save her niece.

And she thinks I'm the surgeon for the job.

I've never mixed business with pleasure.

But the rules no longer apply.

Samara doesn't know it yet, but as soon as I heal her niece's heart...

I'm claiming hers.

Samara Lansing

Everyone says Tate Grimes is the best pediatric heart surgeon in Texas.

They didn't warn me that he's gorgeous, bossy, and a little bit cocky too.

I need him to save my niece. I didn't expect to fall for him.

Resisting him is futile.

Yet loving him is terrifying.

I know a thing or two about MCs and the men who cling to them.

One murdered my sister and orphaned my niece.

Tate swears he's different, and every instinct tells me it's the truth.

But trusting him to fix my niece's heart is one thing.

Can I really trust him to care for mine too?

PROLOGUE

Samara

"Ms. Lansing?"

I glance up from the square section of gray carpeting at my feet, my bleary gaze landing on a blonde in cheerful pink scrubs with brightly colored rubber ducks stamped across them. She gives me a kind smile, her blue eyes full of sympathy.

"That's me," I say, roughly clearing my throat.

"I'm Carly," the blonde says. "I'm here to take you back to meet your niece."

I nod mutely, a little afraid I might cry if I try to say anything else. Until forty-eight hours ago, I didn't even know I had a niece. My older sister,

Siobhan, rarely shared much of her life with me. After our mom died three years ago, I resented her for that. I felt like she abandoned me. Now, I find myself questioning everything I thought I knew. Why didn't she just come back home? Was it her choice to keep me in the dark about her life?

I don't think I'll ever have the answer to those questions now.

"I'll be right here." Troian Bronx, my boss and closest friend, squeezes my hand, letting me know she's here for me. Her bright green eyes shine with empathy.

"Thank you," I whisper, beyond grateful to her for making this trip with me. I'm not sure what I'd do without her. It's been an emotional rollercoaster, and it's nowhere near over. Today, I meet Scout, my six-week-old niece. Tomorrow, we bury her mom. Somewhere between now and then, I process the fact that my niece is gravely ill, and my sister was murdered by a motorcycle club.

I'm not even sure where to begin.

Right here, Samara, I tell myself. *You start right here.* It's the same thing I always tell myself when I'm overwhelmed and under pressure. So far, the mantra has gotten me through every tough day I've faced in my life. It'll just have to get me through this one too.

I'll meet Scout, talk to her doctors, and find out what we're facing. I'll grieve the sister I loved fierce- ly...the one I'm no longer sure I ever really knew at all. How did she get tangled up with a motorcycle club in Texas? I knew Danny Spangler wasn't a good guy, but I never suspected he was in an MC. I never suspected he'd kill my sister and die in a shootout with police either. I would have come to Texas and dragged her out of there myself if I'd known what was happening.

"The PICU is this way," Carly says, her voice soft as she leads me down gayly painted hallways. Children's hospitals are the saddest of all to me. Murals and bright colors meant to soothe the kids just remind parents and caregivers that this is no place for a child. "It can be a little overwhelming, but Miss Scout is a sassy little thing. She's surprised all of us, to be quite honest."

"What..." I clear my throat again. "What's wrong with her heart?"

"Maybe we should wait for the doctors to talk to you," Carly says, hesitation drifting through her eyes.

"Please," I whisper. "No one will tell me anything." I've talked to an army of social workers and police officers over the last two days, but they've danced around Scout's condition, delicately referring to it in euphemisms that only worry me more.

Carly hesitates for another minute and then sighs softly. "She has a congenital heart defect known as truncus arteriosus. It means that she was born with only one blood vessel leading out of the heart instead of two."

"Oh." Fear churns in my stomach, souring it. I should have pushed harder for Troian to be allowed to go back with me, hospital rules about immediate family only be damned. Her husband, Gage, is a heart surgeon, and she had a transplant as a kid. If anyone can make sense of whatever medical mumbo jumbo they're about to throw at me, she can. "How bad is it?"

"We should wait for the doctors," Carly says, her voice firmer this time, but not unkind.

"Of course," I mumble, my heart sinking. I follow her blindly down one corridor and then another. We pass through a set of security doors, turn right, and then pass through another set. A blue placard beside the second set announces that we've reached the PICU.

"You'll have to scrub up," Carly says, pointing me toward a sink.

She follows me over and instructs me on how to properly scrub up nearly to my elbows. Once she's satisfied, we cross to another set of doors. These open automatically. Organized chaos ensues as soon as they do. The unit is organized in little pods with glass walls and doors between them. A nurse sits between every two, monitoring the patients inside. Alarms and equipment beep all over the unit, with doctors, nurses, and support staff swiftly moving from pod to pod.

Unlike the rest of the hospital, there are no murals or happy paintings here. Everything is subdued, designed for function and expediency more than comfort. The sight tugs at my heartstrings. No hospital is a place for small children and infants, but a critical care unit like this is even less so. The nurse's station in the center is brightly lit, but the individual rooms are darker, allowing the children inside to rest as quietly as possible. Those I can see are all tiny, most not even out of their toddler years.

Carly leads me around the nurse's station toward a room on the right. Wires and machines run this way and that from the metal crib in the center of the room. My breath catches in my throat when I see the baby sleeping peacefully in the center. My heart beats against my breastbone in jarring thuds I feel all the way into the soles of my feet. Her shock of raven-black hair...her pale, porcelain skin...those long, long eyelashes.... She looks just like Siobhan.

I move toward the crib on silent feet, my gaze riveted to the angel inside. She's so tiny. I can't even make sense of the jumble of wires hooked up to her. She has oxygen cannulas in her nose with a thin tube running down her right nostril. Tape and a board hold IVs in place on her arm and right leg. A pulse-ox monitor wraps around one tiny toe. Even with the oxygen, her lips have a blue tinge to them. Her skin is all but translucent, her ribs visible with every labored breath she takes.

My eyes water at the sight, a lump rising in my throat.

"She's sedated," Carly says, coming up beside me. "It helps keep her comfortable."

Comfortable for what? I want to ask...but I don't. I already know.

She's dying.

Defiance rises swiftly, stirring in my soul like a battle cry. She's just a baby, an innocent little girl who just lost her mom and her dad—even if he doesn't deserve to be mourned. God or fate or the universe has taken enough from her. The world doesn't get to take more from her. It doesn't get to take her. I won't allow it.

She's mine to watch over now. And I'm not going to lie her die.

I'll save her, Siobhan, I vow silently, tears slipping unchecked down my cheeks. *I promise you; I'll find a way to save your baby girl.*

Chapter One

Tate

One Week Later

"You're calling early," I say, hitting the button on my navigation menu to answer Jason "Cash" Montoya's call. It's not even six-thirty yet. At this hour, he's usually still wrapped up in his girl, Hadley, unaware the rest of the world exists. Since he fell in love and got married, he tends to stay that way. He's head over heels for his pregnant wife.

I give him grief about it at every available opportunity, but the truth is...part of me envies the hell out of him. Waking up alone is getting old. But I've been married to my job for so long I haven't ever put much time or attention into looking for a woman to share my life with. I keep putting it off, figuring I'll get to it one day. Except *one day* never seems to come.

The simple fact is, there isn't anyone in Silver Spoon Falls who interests me enough to want to change my life. If she's in Houston, I haven't run into her there either. So I keep my life the way it is, unwilling to change it just because everyone gives me shit about being single at my age. I spend most of my time dealing with overwrought parents and critically ill children. What free time I have is spent with my MC brothers, dealing with our pain in the ass prospect, or catching up on sleep. I don't have time to dive into dating...especially with someone I don't see myself settling down with.

When I meet the one for me, I'll know it. Until then, I'm perfectly content single. My dad, world-renowned photographer Sage Grimes, was older than I am now when he met my mom at a photoshoot in New York. He knew right away that she was the one. I grew up watching them fall in love time and time again. My dad kissing on her all the time drove me nuts as a kid. Now that I'm older, I appreciate it a helluva lot more. They're blissfully in love and don't care who knows it.

I figure if I can't have the kind of love they have, I don't want it at all.

After all, settling isn't what I do. Neither are half-measures.

There's a reason I'm one of the best pediatric heart surgeons in the country at thirty-six years old. I go after what I want, and I don't stop until it's mine. Cash would call me a stubborn pain in the ass. I prefer driven, motivated. I may have grown up with a silver spoon in my mouth, but my parents' money didn't get me where I am today. Did it help? Of course. I know I had opportunities and privilege a lot of others didn't. But I put myself through medical school. I built my practice from the ground up. I didn't accept my dad's money when he offered, or anyone else's. I wanted to make a name for myself on my own, just like my dad did.

I'm stubborn like that.

"I'd rather be in bed," Cash mutters, "but I've got shit to do today."

I smirk at his surly tone, not surprised he's pissed about it. He owns an investment firm. He's also the President of the Silver Spoon MC, our MC. Between running his company, running the MC, handling our pain in the ass Prospect, and worrying about his pregnant wife, he has more than his fair share to keep him busy these days. Hadley was in an accident a few weeks ago that really shook him up.

"Me too," I say, rolling to a stop at the light on Broadway. "My schedule is packed with patients."

"You're back at work?"

"I've been back," I snort. "Taking care of shit while you were busy taking care of Hadley was overtime."

"I'm not paying you. Consider it payback for you giving us the plague," Cash bitches.

"It was a virus." And it was almost three months ago.

"That you whined about more than anyone."

"Whatever," I mutter, though he's not entirely wrong. Doctors make terrible patients. It's a statistical fact. We're good at healing other people, not at being sick ourselves. But I'm not admitting that to my best friend. He gives me enough grief as it is. "Did you just call to give me more shit?"

"No. I called to tell you that we're giving Rulie and Gloria a bonus."

"We?" My brows rise. Rulie Davis, Cash's PA, is our MC's equivalent of a graybeard. His old lady, Gloria, keeps the clubhouse in order for us. They're family to everyone in the MC, but I get the distinct impression that this *we* Cash speaks of doesn't include the rest of our brothers.

"We," Cash confirms. "As in me and you, motherfucker. I paid for their vacation. You can help pay for the bonus."

"Fuck, fine," I bitch, though I'm not even mad about it. Rulie and Gloria have been managing both of our lives for long enough...ours and everyone else's in the MC. If anyone deserves a bonus after putting up with our shit for this long, they do. Especially after that damn virus went through the club. Men make terrible patients. It's precisely why I work with kids.

"That was suspiciously easy," Cash remarks as if he expected me to put up a fight.

"They deserve a bonus," I say, letting off the brake when the light turns green. I roll through the intersection and then take the next left, headed toward my office next to the hospital downtown. This early, I'm the only one on the road. "Especially since they have to watch your big ass trying to feel Hadley up every five minutes whenever she's at the clubhouse."

"Man, fuck you," he says, laughing. "You're just jealous the only thing warming your bed is that goddamn ego of yours."

"My ego and I sleep just fine. And we don't have to share the covers."

"We both know you're full of shit," he says. "But I'm going to let you run with that line while I'm living my best life with my wife, and you're running through lotion like it's going out of style, fucker."

"I don't use lotion. I prefer the lube I found in your drawer. Speaking of which, you do know that foreplay isn't optional for women, right?" I ask, pulling into the parking lot of my building. A gray Fiat parked in front of the building catches my attention. I'm not sure if it's broken down or if someone just left it overnight, but the California tags stick out. We don't see many of those this far outside of Houston. "I believe the proper medical term is *lick it before you stick it.* Do it well enough, and you won't need the lube."

"I'm not even going to dignify that with a response," Cash says, laughing. "Asshole."

I grin, circling around to the back of the building. "I'll bring you a check later."

"Yeah, later," he says and then disconnects.

My chuckle dies when I see that my nurse, Jules, is already here. I've told her a thousand times that she doesn't have to be in until 7:30, but she never listens. She never listens when I tell her to park by the doors if she's going to insist on coming in this early, either. Jules does what she wants to do, my rules be damned. She's a spitfire with a heart as big as this state.

I'm not sure if she adopted me or if I adopted her, but somewhere along the way, she became like a sister to me. Like my older sister, Sariah, she loves trying to tell me what to do. Unlike when Sariah does it, I actually pay Jules for her input. She's a hell of a nurse.

"You're late," she says as soon as I step through the doors.

"No, you're early." I narrow my eyes on her. "Again."

"Nope." She smacks me in the chest with a folder, smirking. "You have a surgery consult this morning, remember?"

"What consult?" I scowl at the folder.

"The one you told Gage you'd take," she reminds me, referring to my best friend from medical school, Gage Bronx.

"Shit," I curse, taking the folder from her. He called me about it a couple of days ago, said the baby has a congenital defect and is too sick to be flown home to California for the surgery. He asked me to take it as a personal favor. The aunt is his wife's best friend. "That's today?"

"Yep." Jules eyes me critically, her dark gaze scrutinizing my appearance. "You might want to do something with your hair. And put on your coat. You look like you just left the gym."

"That's because I just left the gym," I mutter, tucking the folder under my arm. "I thought I had a few minutes to deal with some notes this morning before I started seeing patients."

"No such luck. You need to call your twin after your consult, and then call Sheriff Armstrong." Her nose wrinkles. "He called you four times yesterday about Brady. I don't like him, by the way."

"No one likes Brady." The Prospect has been nothing but a pain in the collective ass of the MC since we agreed to do his brother, the Mayor, a solid. Lesson learned. Next time, we'll be burning that bridge and saving ourselves the headache.

Unlike a lot of MCs, ours isn't involved with anything illegal. We expect all our members to be legitimate. No criminal history, no bullshit. Brady failed to disclose his criminal history, which had Dillon Armstrong knocking on our door with an arrest warrant for him a few months ago. Getting it sorted out has been a pain in the ass. Brady is lucky Cash wanted to keep the mayor on his good side or we would have helped Armstrong cuff him.

"Xavier called?" My twin brother is supposed to be in Japan, working some big deal for our mom's company. At least he was two days ago. He went so our father could whisk her off to Europe for a week. Both he and Sariah work for her company. She'll be handing it over to them soon. She keeps insisting on naming me to the board as well, but I'll be a silent partner. I have no interest in running the company.

"Yep. He wants you to call him later. And I wasn't talking about Brady. I meant Sheriff Armstrong," Jules says, rolling her eyes at me. She tosses her head, causing her ponytail to bounce as if to emphasize her annoyance with the Sheriff. "He's bossy."

"He's the Sheriff."

"He doesn't have to be a tyrant about it."

I arch a brow, amused. "He's the Sheriff. I'm pretty sure that's in the job description."

"Overgrown, bossy, growly..." Jules mumbles a few other descriptors under her breath before the phone rings, snagging her attention. She snaps out of her diatribe, settling her irritated gaze on me. "Go put your doctor clothes on. We have things to do."

"You do remember that I'm the one who pays you, right?" I call after her, and then chuckle when she throws a hand up in the air in response. "Guess she's not a fan of Dillon Armstrong," I mutter to myself.

Huh. I wonder what he said to ruffle her feathers this morning? He's not a bad guy. In fact, he's one of the most levelheaded men I know. If he's in a mood bad enough to rile Jules, I'm guessing whatever Brady did isn't something I want to deal with today.

I shrug it off, deciding someone else can handle Brady for the day, and head toward my office to change and look over the new patient's file before her aunt arrives. Gage didn't have a lot of details when he called. All I really know is that the baby is young and has a congenital heart defect. Her aunt is her legal guardian, which is a recent development.

I toss the file toward my desk, reaching to pull my t-shirt off over my head. Then and only then do I realize there's a woman curled up on the sofa across from my desk, one hand tucked beneath her cheek. She's passed out, her plump lips softly parted.

I freeze with my arms halfway over my head, staring in shock.

She's...Jesus. I drop my arms back to my sides and blink, trying to process the chaos currently coursing through me. A landslide roars through me, toppling entire sections of my soul in its wake. My heart pounds a frenetic, dizzying rhythm, the throb of my cock beating in syncopation. There's something about her...something so *familiar* and yet I'd stake my life on the fact that I've never met her before in my life.

She's tiny, curled up into a little ball on the sofa as if to make herself as small as possible. Even that doesn't hide the lush curves of her body from my gaze. The swells of her breasts rising and falling with each deep breath she takes, the generous flare of her hips...the thickness of her thighs. She can't be any older than twenty-two or twenty-three, but she has the ripe, luscious body of a woman a decade older.

Her hair is a strange mix of deep browns and black, the kind women pay a fortune for at the salon. But I don't think hers came from a box or a colorist. It fits her too well. *Everything* about her fits her too well, from her beautiful body to her sun-kissed skin to her adorable pout. Dark brows crinkle in her sleep before smoothing again. Her round cheeks are pink, as if she's dreaming things she shouldn't be. It makes me curious as hell to know what's going on behind those closed eyes. Her eyes.... What color are they? Brown? Green? Blue? The fact that I don't already know bothers me.

I watch her for a long moment, my feet rooted in place.

She's a masterpiece. Every little part of her is utter perfection, as if it were handcrafted specifically to check every one of my boxes. And my dick has never been this hard in my life.

I feel like an asshole for staring at her, thinking filthy thoughts about her...yet the civilized part of my brain short circuited, leaving some primal, predatory part in charge. That part... *Christ*, that part likes every filthy thought currently running through my head. This angel on her knees with my dick between her lips. Her bent over my desk with that long hair wrapped around my fist... Those pouty lips crying out my name while I pump into her from behind.

Tate. Tate. Oh god, harder please.

Ah, hell.

I turn on my heel and flee the room like the hounds of hell are nipping at my heels.

"There's a woman in my office," I growl as soon as I find Jules at her desk.

She lifts her gaze from her computer screen, staring at me levelly.

"*Why* is there a woman in my office?"

"We already had this conversation, Tate," she says, looking at me like I'm crazy.

"We most definitely did not fucking talk about the woman sleeping in my office," I growl, glaring at her. "I think I'd remember that."

"Aww, she's sleeping?"

"Jules!"

"Tate!"

I pinch the bridge of my nose. "Why is there a woman sleeping in my office?"

"Uh, because she's tired?" Jules gives me another look that says she's questioning my intelligence. "It's not even seven and she drove in from Houston to meet you this morning. She's probably exhausted, poor thing. I think she's been sleeping in the waiting room at the hospital."

She's been sleeping in a waiting room? Why is my blood pressure rising at the thought of her sleeping in the waiting room?

"She drove here from Houston this morning?"

Jules nods.

Fucking hell. She *is* exhausted.

"You could have warned me she was in my office," I mutter without heat.

"I told you that you had a consult."

"I thought you meant later."

"Did I say you had a consult later? No. I said you were late."

"Shit."

"You're cursing an awful lot this morning."

I huff out a curse and then turn a sharp glare on Jules before she can comment on it. She holds up her hands in a gesture of surrender, pressing her lips together in a tight line as if to indicate she's not going to say a word. I'm almost positive she's only doing it to keep from laughing at me, but I let that slide.

I need to go wake Sleeping Beauty. Jules can give me shit about my language later. Preferably after I process how absolutely fucked I am. Because the woman sleeping in my office? I'm pretty sure *interest* doesn't even begin to cover how I feel about her right now. Judging by the voice currently roaring *mine* like a demon, interest doesn't cover it by half.

"What's her name?"

"Her name is Samara Lansing," Jules says.

Samara Lansing. It suits her. The first name, anyway.

We'll work on changing the last name to mine after I save her niece.

CHAPTER TWO

Samara

"**S**leeping Beauty."

Something drifts across the side of my face. I groan, lifting my hand to bat it away. I'm warm and comfortable and I don't want to move, let alone wake up and deal with whatever crisis awaits me today. There have been a lot of those lately. I'm so tired. I can't remember the last time I slept for more than a couple of hours at a time.

"Wake up, Sleeping Beauty."

"It's too early," I complain, squeezing my eyes closed as if that'll make whoever is annoying me go away and stop interrupting my dream. I was on the beach, my toes in the sand, the rays of the hot California sun spilling down over me while waves crashed against the shoreline.

"Trust me, angel, I'm aware."

The amusement bleeding through the deep rumble of his voice breaks through the haze in my mind. The last lingering rays of the California sun slip away. The gentle crash of water against wet earth recedes, taking the feel of the sand beneath my feet with it.

I'm on a plush sofa, my hand tucked beneath my cheek, my neck bent at an odd angle.

This isn't the hospital.

I fly into a sitting position with a gasp.

"There you are."

I blink rapidly at the man crouched in front of me, trying to jolt my mind into motion. For a long moment, nothing comes. I just stare into the darkest green eyes I've ever seen in my life, my mind wiped clean. I'm not sure if it's the lack of sleep, if it's him, or if it's both causing the reaction. But I think it's him.

He's beautiful. His dark hair is damp and messy as if he recently showered and then ran his hands through it. A day's worth of stubble surrounds his full lips, softening his razor-sharp jawline. Intelligence and humor shine in his eyes as they track slowly across my face.

"Gold," he murmurs, one corner of his lips crooking upward.

"What?"

"Your eyes are gold."

"They're hazel."

I have no idea who he is or where I am, yet I instinctively know that I'm safe with him. I see that truth burning in his eyes—safety, security, sanctuary. Protection blazes in the emerald depths, searing me with softness and intensity in equal measures. So does something else...*possession*. The flames of it caress my skin like a kiss as his eyes document every feature of my face. From the scar on my forehead to the little freckles scattered across the bridge of my nose to the dimple in my right cheek, he misses nothing. His gaze roves downward, taking in my rumpled hoodie, wrinkled jeans, and ballet flats.

I steal another peek at him, trying to figure out who he is. He's gorgeous, there's no denying that. The white coat hanging open over his broad shoulders and the stethoscope peeking from around his neck finally jogs my brain into motion. Realization dawns with a powerful lurch.

"Dr. Grimes!" I blurt, relief rushing through me...followed immediately by the sting of embarrassment. This is Dr. Grimes, the pediatric heart surgeon Troian and her husband, Gage, sent me to see. I must have fallen asleep on the couch in his office waiting for our meeting. "I'm so sorry. I must have dozed off. Oh my gosh. What time is it?" I press my hands to my red cheeks, trying to calm my racing heart.

"Easy, Samara," he croons, reaching out to place a hand on my arm. An electric charge shoots from his palm to my skin, startling both of us. His gaze tangles with mine again. There's something calming about him...and something a little bit wild too. He's a lion. They're beautiful, powerful, and confident. They even seem peaceful when they're lounging on the rocks, bathing in the sun. But provoke one and you might live long enough to regret it.

This man isn't like any of the doctors I've met this week. There's nothing staid or ordinary about him. Nothing *safe*. He's an apex predator and he knows it...but his eyes are soft, his expression full of empathy. All week, I've been floundering out of my depth, trying to understand complex medical problems I knew nothing about until a week ago. I've felt the sharp edge of judgement and the arrogant, condescending looks cast my way. Yet this man catches me sleeping in his office and still treats me with gentleness.

For a long moment, neither of us speaks. We just stare at one another again, his scent clouding my mind. It's leather and citrus. The combination is far more erotic than it should be.

Who am I kidding? *Everything* about this man is erotic as hell. I was expecting a middle-aged, bespectacled man with thinning hair and a perfunctory manner. This man is sex on legs.

"Um, I'm sorry I fell asleep," I whisper, trying to force that thought out of my head. It doesn't matter what Dr. Grimes looks like, how good he smells, or how hard my heart is pounding right now. It doesn't even matter that part of me wants to feel his hand on my skin again. All that matters is Scout. Gage and Troian trust this man to save her life.

"Jules said you drove in from Houston this morning." His dark brows furrow. "Had I known, we could have scheduled this meeting for later in the day."

"My niece has some tests later today," I explain, fidgeting though I don't know why. I don't owe him an explanation. One tumbles out anyway. "This was the only time in my schedule."

He eyes me for a minute, his expression softening with understanding. "You've been staying at the hospital with your niece."

"I'm her legal guardian."

"Her parents?"

A fresh wave of grief wells up before I can shove it back down. All week, I've been waiting for someone to ask outright about Siobhan and Danny, but no one has. They judge without facts, chalk my sister up to a bad mom who made bad decisions, and refer to her death in euphemisms as if that makes it more palatable. Hearing this man ask brings it all roaring back to the surface.

"They're dead," I whisper past the lump in my throat. "It happened a little over a week ago."

"Shit," he curses, regret flaring in his eyes. "I'm sorry. I didn't realize..."

"It's fine," I lie, waving off his apology. I wave off the grief too, pushing it back down to deal with later. I'll cry when I'm alone in the shower like I do every night. It's the only time to myself I have these days. Every other minute of my day is spent with complete strangers in waiting rooms or the cafeteria or at Scout's bedside.

"Do you need a minute?"

"No." I quickly shake my head. "I need to get back as soon as possible."

He nods and rises to his feet.

I swallow hard. Lord, he's big. Not overweight just...*big.* He's maybe six-three with broad shoulders and a barrel chest. He looks more like a football player than a heart surgeon. Then again, Gage was an actor before he went to medical school...and I lived in a tiny trailer in the middle of nowhere before landing my dream job writing game apps for

Troian's family's company. We all have lives and pasts, don't we? We all came from somewhere and we're all going somewhere.

Most of us, I amend silently, thinking about Siobhan again.

"Come on, Sleeping Beauty," Dr. Grimes says, holding out a hand to me. "Let's move to my desk and we'll talk about your niece."

I hesitate for a second and then place my hand in his. As soon as he touches me, that same electrical spark shoots up my arm. He feels it too and grits his teeth, letting out a soft curse. I stumble when he pulls me up, nearly bumping into him before I catch myself. He steadies me with a hand on my waist.

"Jesus, you're tiny," he mutters.

"Am not," I whisper, something soft washing through me. No one has ever accused me of being tiny. Short, yes. I'm barely five-three. But I'm thick and curvy and have been my whole life. I like the sound of this man calling me tiny though. Maybe I shouldn't. Maybe I need him to see me as strong and capable and powerful, but something about him seeing me as delicate doesn't immediately make me want to smash the patriarchy.

"Yeah, you are." He tips his head down toward mine, his expression soft. "How old are you, Samara?"

"Old enough to provide for Scout." I've already been through the whole spiel with the social worker assigned the Scout's case.

"Good to know," he says, leaning closer. There are flecks of jade in his eyes. "But that's not why I'm asking. I'm not questioning your ability to care for your niece. How old are you?"

"Twenty-two."

"You're young."

"I could say the same about you," I remind him, trying not to stare at his lips. His cologne is making me dizzy. Or maybe it's just him. "I've seen a lot of doctors this week. None of them look like you."

His lips tip up into that crooked grin again. "You know what makes me a hell of a doctor?"

"What?" I whisper, completely transfixed by this man. There's something about him that's just...spellbinding. I want to lean in closer, enfold myself into his personal space, and let his shadow embrace me. I want to let *him* hold me until my world makes sense again.

No. No way, Samara. He's going to be Scout's surgeon. That's it.

"My age," he says, his deep voice whisper soft. Somehow, his eyes seem to whisper too, though I don't even know how that's possible. "I've got steady hands and a stubborn streak a mile wide. I decided when I was still a kid that I wanted to save other kids, so that's what I've dedicated my whole life to doing. I'm one of the best pediatric heart surgeons in the country because I *wanted* to be one of the best. I didn't learn through trial and error or because wisdom comes with age. I learned because I wanted to learn, understand?"

"That's what Gage, um, Dr. Bronx said," I say. He swore that if anyone could save Scout's life, this man could. He was confident of that fact. I've known Gage since I started working for Troian two years ago. He doesn't make promises he can't keep.

"He said I was a stubborn bastard, didn't he?" Dr. Grimes asks, his grin growing.

"Maybe."

The deep rumble of his laugh washes through me. My nipples tighten as a frisson of heat dances in my lower belly. His voice is incredible but that laugh? *Wow.*

"Come on," he says, leading me toward his desk.

Only then do I realize he's still holding onto my hand. He doesn't look like he plans to let it go, so I follow behind him, quickly trying to smooth my hair into order with my free hand. It probably didn't do much good. I didn't come dressed to impress today. I came prepared for another long day of meetings and sitting around the hospital.

Maybe that's for the best. I don't need to impress Dr. Grimes. I need him to save my niece. Anything beyond that is out of the question. My entire life just changed. The last thing I need is to complicate it by falling for a doctor in Texas, especially one who looks like this. He probably has women beating down his door trying to get a date with him. I haven't been on a date since Thad Porter took me to Prom my senior year of high school four years ago.

Our date ended with him puking in the bushes after drinking half the flask of bourbon my mom gave him. He spent the next two weeks avoiding me anytime we passed each other in the hallway. And I moved out of my mom's house as soon as I graduated. If she wanted to drink herself to an early grave, I wasn't going to stay and watch it happen. I just didn't expect it to happen so soon. I wasn't even gone a full year before she wrapped her car around a light pole.

Siobhan came home for the funeral. It was the last time I saw her.

"Have a seat," Dr. Grimes says.

I drop down into the seat across from his desk, folding my hands together in my lap.

He circles around to the other side and pulls out his chair.

"Tell me about your niece," he orders me, reaching for a folder on top of the desk.

"Her name is Scout Lansing," I say. "She's seven and a half weeks old," I explain her diagnosis to him the way it was explained to me...the fact that she only has one vessel leading out of her heart instead of two and the hole between the bottom chambers of her heart. "She, um, she's not doing well."

"Why wasn't the initial surgery performed earlier?" he asks, glancing up from her file.

"They didn't know about the defect until recently," I say, glancing down at my hands to avoid his reaction. I've seen a thousand variations of it over the last week. "She wasn't born in a hospital."

"It didn't show up on prenatal screenings?"

"There weren't any prenatal visits after the first trimester."

Dr. Grimes is quiet for a moment. His silence speaks volumes, the same volumes I've been reading all week from every other man in a white coat I've sat across from. Siobhan wouldn't have cared what any of them thought about her. She never did. It's the only thing that's kept me from shouting out the truth this week. But this time, I find myself unable to remain silent while stones fly at Siobhan's memory. I care what this man thinks, though I'm not sure why. Because he's Gage's friend? Because I actually like him? I don't know.

"My sister was a good mom," I whisper, my throat raw with emotion. "She loved Scout. But Scout's father was in a motorcycle club. My sister found out the club was trafficking women. She...um, she was helping them escape and the club caught her. They kept her under guard after that. She managed to get Scout out a little over a week ago to get her help but..." I trail off and swallow hard, unable to finish the sentence. "Before you judge her or her situation, you should know that much about her."

"Look at me, Samara," he says, his voice soft.

I reluctantly lift my gaze to his.

"Your sister was a fucking warrior," he growls, his eyes glittering with sincerity.

"Thank you," I whisper, biting my lip to keep from crying.

He watches me for a moment, his expression soft. "You said Scout's father was in an MC?"

"Yeah."

"Do you think all motorcycle clubs are like his, Samara? That they're all outlaws who hurt women like your sister?"

"At the end of the day, it doesn't really matter, does it?" I ask, not sure why he cares what I think. Until recently, I never put much thought into MCs or the kind of men drawn to them. Now though? Well, it's hard to look compassionately on the kind of men who killed my sister and orphaned my niece. Had Siobhan not risked her life to save her daughter, it would have been Scout's funeral we attended last week instead of my sister's. They would have let an innocent baby die just to keep my sister from spilling their dirty secrets. If those are the type of men who cling to MCs, they aren't men at all.

"Answer the question," Dr. Grimes says.

"It doesn't matter if they call themselves outlaws or not," I say, holding his gaze. "Whether they run drugs or guns or women or pretend to play by the law, they're willing to kill—and die—for a patch on their vest and a brotherhood that ends as soon as one steps out of line. They're cut from the same cloth, regardless of how they try to neaten it up."

His brows furrow, a shadow passing through his expression. But he quickly blinks it away and flips Scout's file closed. "I'll perform the surgery," he says, meeting my gaze. "But I want something from you in exchange."

"I can pay you," I say, frowning. "I'm not here to ask you to do the surgery for free." Troian has been working with the insurance company all week to pull off a miracle and ensure they'll cover as much of the surgery as possible. My savings should cover the rest. I'm not the poor girl who grew up in a run-down trailer anymore. Thanks to my job, I'm more than capable of taking care of Scout and myself.

"I'm not concerned about the money, angel," he says, something...possessive in his gaze again. I like the sight of it far too much. "I don't want you sleeping in the waiting room anymore."

"I'm not leaving Scout."

"You won't be leaving her," he assures me. "I have an apartment right across Main Street. You'll have full use of it while she's in the hospital. You'll stay there at night so you're getting actual sleep."

"I can't do that."

"You can."

"I can't."

"You can," he says, narrowing his eyes on me. "You aren't going to be any good to your niece if you're falling over in exhaustion. This isn't a sprint. Until she's strong enough to move here, you need more than a chair in a waiting room."

"H-here?" I gape at him, certain I'm hearing things. "We're going back to California once she's strong enough."

"No," he says quietly, his gaze firm. "You're not. She's going to need continued monitoring and follow-up. It'll be a year, maybe longer before you're able to return to California, and then she'll need additional surgeries as she grows. You're here for the long haul."

"I..." I blink at him, trying to absorb this news.

"Welcome home, Sleeping Beauty," he murmurs, throwing my world completely out of orbit. He's not just talking about Texas. I'm not even sure he's talking about Silver Spoon Falls. Part of me gets the distinct impression that by *home* he means right here with him.

I'm going to strangle Gage.

CHAPTER THREE

Tate

"Let me get this straight," Jude "Fifth" Despora says, his deep voice a rough growl of sound. "Her sister was murdered by an MC, you moved her into your place, and failed to mention that you're the VP of an MC?"

"Something like that," I mutter, jogging up the steps toward the glass doors of the luxury high rise across Main Street from Texas Children's. Located in south-central Houston, the Texas Medical Center campus is the largest medical complex in the world. It sprawls across two square miles of the city, housing twenty-one different hospitals, a plethora of medical institutions, and various associated facilities.

Apartment buildings like this one have cropped up all over the place, making it easier for the people who work here and the families seeking care to get from A to B without having to commute in. I keep an apartment here for days when I'm too beat to make the drive back to Silver Spoon Falls after seeing patients at the hospital here...which happens often. My primary practice is in Silver Spoon Falls, but the hospital there simply isn't equipped to handle some of my more fragile pediatric cases. I perform a lot of surgeries here and hold a heart clinic once a week as well. I end up spending a good portion of my time in Houston.

"You're making me look bad," Fifth complains. He's a lawyer, hence the road name. He likes to plead the fifth whenever he thinks it'll keep him out of trouble. It rarely works outside of the courtroom. He may be a suave bastard, but we know him too well to fall for it. "All this time, I've been telling everyone I'm the third smartest man in the club behind you and Hacker. Clearly, I've been over-estimating your intelligence and underestimating mine."

"Asshole," I mutter, laughing. "I have a plan."

"To frighten her off? Because that's precisely what you're going to do," he warns me, his disapproval loud and clear. "If she has a problem with MCs, lying by omission isn't going to win you any points with her, Hands. You know it as well as I do."

"I'm not lying by omission," I say, ducking through the door when the doorman holds it open for me. "I'm doling out the truth in pieces that make it more easily digestible for a traumatized woman who just lost her sister to a bunch of assholes."

"You're so full of shit, for a minute there, you almost sounded like a politician," Fifth snorts.

"Well, if it isn't a lawyer calling the kettle black," I drawl, leaning up against a column to wait for Samara. Fifth's moral compass points firmly north. If Cash is the heart of our brotherhood, Fifth is our conscience. He keeps us all in line, makes sure we keep our noses clean and our heads on straight, but I give him hell about being a lawyer anyway. It keeps him humble.

Even without him to keep us on the straight and narrow, we aren't what Samara thinks. Not a single man in our club would kill—or die—for the patch on our cuts but for the men who earned it. We're brothers. Family. That doesn't make us criminals. We're doctors, lawyers, CEOs. Hell, Bender is a rockstar. Angel is actual royalty, a prince. But Samara has been through hell, and I don't blame her for judging MCs harshly. In her position, I'm not sure anyone else would feel any differently than she does right now.

An MC just killed her sister. They nearly killed an innocent child. Every single motherfucker involved deserves to fry for what they did. But we aren't them or anything like them. The best way I know how to prove that to Samara is by showing her who we are. I have no intentions of keeping the truth from her. I'm just going to give it to her in small doses. I don't want her running anywhere but to me. That'll just piss me off.

I can't even fucking explain it. Before she even looked at me, I felt her in my soul. The minute those gold eyes finally settled on me, something started roaring that she's mine. It hasn't stopped roaring ever since. As soon as I heal her niece's heart, I'm claiming hers. I'm not a man who loses, especially when it counts. I'll be damned if I lose this time. Samara and her niece are mine now. God help anyone who thinks different.

"Asshole," Fifth says, chuckling and then he sobers. "Since you clearly didn't call for my advice, I'm guessing you called to have me look into her sister's death? See what I can find out?"

"I'd appreciate it," I murmur.

"What do you have?"

"Her name was Siobhan Lansing. She died a little over a week ago outside of Dallas. Baby's father was a Danny Spangler," I say, relaying what little I know. Samara didn't fill me in on many details, and I didn't ask. When she tells me the full story, I don't want it to be because I demanded answers. I want it to be because she trusts me to hold her while she grieves the sister she obviously loved a great deal. She doesn't trust me right now, not with this.

I can't say I blame her for that, either. I know how fucking judgmental doctors are, how pretentious they can be. They've probably sat across from her all week, staring down their noses at her, accusation in their eyes when they discuss Scout's condition and how she should have had this surgery weeks ago. I'm guessing not one of them considered that it wasn't Siobhan's choice not to seek medical care during her pregnancy or after. I'm guessing not one of them knows she sacrificed her life to get her daughter to safety. I doubt they looked far enough into her case to find out.

It grates on my nerves to think of how many times Samara has had to bear the judgement of men who don't even understand true sacrifice. Her sister was a warrior, and so is she. Her entire world just changed and she's still standing. She's still fighting for her sister's memory and the baby she left behind. She's stronger at twenty-two than most men could ever hope to be, but I don't think she even realizes it. She's in survival mode, just trying to make it from minute to minute.

I've seen it a thousand times. When your kid is sick, nothing else matters. Scout might not be hers by birth, but she's going to be a hell of an aunt to that baby girl. She hasn't left her side all week.

I talked to Scout's care team this afternoon. I read her chart from cover to cover too. She's dangerously ill, but she's a fighter too. Her team is relieved I'm taking over. Dr. Shapiro is a good surgeon, but good isn't enough in a case like this. Scout doesn't need good. She needs the best. She needs me. Dr. Shapiro knows it as well as I do.

"I'll see what I can find out for you," Fifth says.

"Thanks, man."

"No problem. Good luck."

I disconnect and shove my phone into my pocket to wait for Samara.

Within five minutes, she ducks through the door, buried so deep in her hoodie she looks like she's in the Siberian wilderness instead of Houston in July. Her dark hair blows all around her face before she manages to bat it back into place, making me smile. She's fucking beautiful without even trying. She looks like she's headed to the gallows instead of standing in a luxury high rise.

I offered to meet her at the hospital, but she insisted on meeting me here instead. I don't think she wants anyone to know she's staying at my place. As if they aren't all going to know soon enough anyway. I plan to ensure they know she's mine. They won't be treating her with anything less than the respect she deserves, or they'll answer to me, plain and simple. Fuck their rules and their judgement.

"Hey," she says when she spots me. Her gaze dances up and down my body, her cheeks heating before she quickly glances down at her at shoes. Fuck, I like how sweet she gets when she's feeling shy. I can't wait to see her looking at me the same way when she's spread across my bed, wearing nothing but a smile and my love bites. My dick stiffens at the thought.

"You cold, angel?" I ask, grinning at her.

"I'm always cold," she says, scrunching up her nose at me. "I thought Texas was supposed to be horrible in the summer."

"It's eighty-five degrees outside. That's flip-flop weather." I push away from the column, strolling toward her.

"It's ninety in San Diego," she says, craning her neck back to look up at me.

My smile grows when her little nose turns up, as if to punctuate her feelings about the inferiority of Texas weather. I happen to agree with her on that front. My mom runs a successful modeling agency for plus-size models in Los Angeles. My siblings and I grew up in Beverly Hills. I didn't move to Texas until I started my residency at Baylor. The weather sucks, especially when the humidity kicks in, but the rest of the state isn't so bad. It's home to me now.

"Come on," I murmur, leading her to the elevator with a hand on the small of her back. "Let's go up and get you settled."

She mumbles something under her breath that sounds like a complaint, but she doesn't speak again until we're on the elevator. As soon as the doors close behind us, she scurries to the far corner. Her brows furrow when I swipe my keyfob and press the button for the top floor.

"I thought you said you had an apartment here."

"I do."

"A penthouse isn't an apartment."

"It's a penthouse apartment."

She huffs at me. "I should really be paying you rent if I'm going to be staying here, Dr. Grimes."

"Tate."

"What?" The little groove between her brows deepens.

"My name is Tate. That's what you call me. Not Dr. Grimes. Tate."

She's a stubborn little thing, I'll give her that. As soon as I say it, her lips compress into a thin line, her gold eyes narrowing further. "I don't think that's very appropriate," she says. "You're my niece's surgeon."

I prowl toward her across the chrome and glass elevator, fighting a smirk when she plasters herself up against the wall like she plans to climb it to avoid me. Once I'm in her personal space, close enough to touch her but not close enough to make her feel like she can't get away from me, I tilt my head down toward her.

"I don't give a fuck if it's appropriate or not, angel," I murmur, skimming my nose along her crown. After spending a week in the hospital with Scout, she should smell like the place, but she doesn't. She smells like coconut and sunshine, like the beach and home. "You'll learn soon enough that I make my own rules. When you're sleeping under my roof, you'll call me Tate."

She makes a soft sound in the back of her throat that turns my dick to steel. That needy whine, that shocked gasp. *Fuck*, I can't wait to rattle this woman and turn every single thing she thinks she knows about doctors and men like me on its head. I'm not like any man she's ever met before. I'm *her* man. Already, I feel the connection between us growing, feel the need to possess and claim this delicate, fierce angel beating at me.

"Back up," she whispers, her voice shaking.

"Not until you call me by my name, Samara."

I'm pushing the bounds of propriety to their breaking point. I know it. She knows it. We both know she could probably have my job for this...but we both know she won't. She wants me too. I saw it lurking in those gold eyes this morning. I see it blazing in them now. She feels the same undeniable pull. She's just afraid to give in to it.

"Say it, baby," I demand on a whisper, running my lips along her crown this time. I'm not sure why I need her to give me this so fucking badly but I do. I don't want to be Dr. Grimes to her, especially not when we're alone.

"Dammit, Tate," she whispers.

I press my lips to her temple in a soft kiss. Her body trembles against mine. Even through her oversized hoodie, I feel how soft she is. "I'm going to save your niece, angel. And while I'm doing that, we're going to get to know each other. Intimately."

"You're Scout's surgeon," she reminds me again.

"And we both know if I slipped my hand inside your panties right now, they'd be soaked for me," I growl, narrowing my eyes on her. "We also know they haven't been that way for any other doctor you've met this week. Or any man in recent memory, have they, Samara?"

"I..."

My warning growl quickly silences whatever lie she was going to tell.

She shakes her head instead, silently agreeing with me.

The elevator shudders to a stop on the top floor. The doors slide open.

Samara startles like a frightened doe.

"Easy, angel," I croon, running a hand down her side. "Easy."

"Easy for you to say," she sniffs, glaring at me. "You didn't just step out of your life and into the *Twilight Zone*."

I chuckle, taking a step back and holding out my hand. "This isn't the *Twilight Zone*. This is your life now that I'm in it. I guess Gage didn't tell you everything about me, did he?"

"I guess not," she mutters, reluctantly letting me pull her from the elevator. "He certainly left out the parts about you being overgrown and bossy."

"Nah, angel. I'm not bossy. I'm *the* boss."

She snorts, shaking her head as a small smile plays at her lips. "Whatever you say, bossy," she says. And then she stops walking and does a double take, gaping at the apartment around us. "Holy crap, Tate. This place is amazing."

I cast a critical eye around, trying to see what she does. The walls are all glass, looking out over the Medical Center to the south and west, and Rice University to the north. Automatic blinds black out the windows with the touch of a button, turning the apartment into a fortress. Thick rugs cover the porcelain floors. Expensive bowls and vases rest on equally as expensive tables. But the furniture is soft and plush, made for comfort more than style.

The truth is, I don't give a shit about impressing anyone when I'm here. I care about sleeping so I'm not useless to the patients fighting for their lives across the street. If I'm not at the top of my game, I'm no use to them. I didn't pick the penthouse because it screams money. I picked it because it's completely soundproofed. Nothing intrudes, allowing me to sleep like the dead.

"It's better than a chair in the waiting room," I murmur. "You'll be able to rest here. And sharing a bathroom with me is a hell of a lot better than sharing it with fifteen random strangers. I clean up after myself, and I have fluffy towels."

"Sh-sharing with you?" She blinks wide eyes at me.

"Mmhmm. There's only one bedroom." I wink at her. "Don't worry though, baby. I won't tell anyone how much you like to cuddle at night."

Her mouth pops open.

I close it with a finger beneath her chin and then brush my thumb over her bottom lip. It's so damn soft. Christ, I can't wait to taste it. "I'm teasing, Samara," I say quietly. "I'll keep my hands to myself until you're ready for me to put them all over that beautiful body of yours."

"I'm killing Gage," she whispers.

"You can't." I tap her on her nose, smiling. "Scout needs you."

"Fine," she huffs. "I'll kill him when she's eighteen."

"Hey, ladybug," Samara whispers, running her palm gently over Scout's head. "I brought a special visitor for you tonight. He's bossy, but he's a doctor, so I guess he can't help it."

I smile at her comment, amused. She's been calling me bossy all evening. I don't mind. She can call me whatever she wants. It doesn't change the facts. I know what I want and what I want is her.

Scout's resting comfortably in her crib, her tiny lips slightly parted. Her skin is ashen and a pale blue from lack of oxygen. It's common with her condition. Because there's only one vessel instead of two, oxygen-rich blood and oxygen-poor blood mix on the way out of the heart, meaning not enough of the former gets to the lungs. Her condition hasn't deteriorated enough for her to require a ventilator just yet but it's close. Without surgery, her health will continue to decline. In a matter of weeks, her lungs simply won't be able to keep up. They'll fail. Eventually, her heart will too.

Congenital defects are a particularly cruel twist of genetics. They form long before science even has a hope of stopping them. By the time most parents even know something is wrong, the course is already set. In Scout's case, even if Siobhan had been tested during pregnancy, the outcome wouldn't have changed. Scout would have been in the operating room sooner, but there is no unraveling a congenital defect.

It seems like she rests a little easier with Samara crooning to her. Her heart rate slows, her tiny body sinking a little deeper into sedation. She's a beautiful little girl, a dark-haired angel like her aunt. My heart pulses with emotion as I watch Samara with her. She's a natural, the fierce love she feels for the tiny baby pouring out of her. It pulses in the air around her, shining as bright as the sun.

Not for the first time today, I find myself awestruck by her. She gave up everything without hesitation to be here for Scout. She's holding it together admirably when anyone else would be broken on the floor.

"Were you and your sister close?" I ask, wanting to understand her. *Needing* to understand her on levels I'm not sure I can put into words.

She freezes for a moment and then slowly relaxes, stroking her hand over Scout's head again. "We were. Once." She sighs. "Siobhan left home my junior year of high school. We kept in touch regularly for the first couple of years, and then things changed. After our mom died, she grew more distant."

"Your mom died?"

She bobs her head in a tired nod. "Three years ago, " she says, her voice soft. "She had too much to drink and decided to get behind the wheel of her car anyway."

I frown, leaning back against the glass wall. "Was this a common occurrence?"

"Common enough."

Jesus.

"Our mom died instantly," she continues after a moment. "Siobhan came home for the funeral. That was the last time I saw her. I tried to convince her to move back after that, but she seemed happy." She huffs out a sad breath. "I should have tried harder."

"Hey." I push away from the wall and cross toward her before gently turning her to face me. "No one can predict the future, angel. Don't force yourself to carry guilt that doesn't belong to you. You didn't know."

"Did she?" she whispers, staring up at me with wide, worried eyes. "I keep asking myself that question, Tate. How long was Danny involved with this club? How long was she involved? I have so many damn questions."

"Then we'll find the answers," I say, pulling her into my arms. Surprisingly, she doesn't fight me. She lets me comfort her. "But I won't allow you to feel guilt that doesn't belong to you. It belongs to the club who did this to her."

"I hate them," she whispers.

"I know." I dig my thumbs into the back of her neck, massaging the tendons. "But not all MCs are the same."

"How do you know?"

Tell her, a little voice whispers. *You have to tell her.*

"Because I'm not," I murmur. "Because my brothers aren't."

She goes rigid in my arms and then pulls back. Her confused gaze meets mine. "What do you mean, you're not?" she asks. "Are you saying that you're in an—?"

"Yes."

Fear trickles into her gold eyes, stopping my heart. Fuck. Seeing it there burns like corrosive acid. The last thing I want is for this incredible woman to fear me or my brothers.

"We're not them, Samara," I say, my voice soft, emphatic.

I'm not sure if she believes me or not. Scout's night nurse bustles in, interrupting us before she can respond.

"Hey, Dr. Grimes. Good evening, Miss Lansing," she says, smiling between us. "It's time for Miss Scout's meds."

Samara stares at me for a long, silent moment and then spins away, her expression indecipherable.

Fuck. I should have stuck to the plan.

CHAPTER FOUR

Samara

"I'm killing your husband," I inform Troian, pacing back and forth in front of the window overlooking Rice University. This late, the University looks more like a park than an institute of higher learning. Aside from a few handfuls of students, the various courtyards are all but empty.

"You can't," Troian says. "I'm not raising his boys alone. They're too much like him."

"He could have warned me that Tate is in a freaking motorcycle gang!"

She laughs quietly. "It's not a gang, Samara."

I grunt, not so sure I agree with her. Whether they call it a club or a gang or something else, it checks the same boxes. Maybe they aren't selling drugs or prostituting women, I don't know. I feel like an idiot for what I said this morning though. He's been nothing but kind to me, and I insulted him and his friends! He probably thinks I'm a bitch. I'm not entirely convinced he's wrong. I'm not entirely convinced he's right either. As soon as he told me the truth, my heart stopped beating.

For the first time since I met him this morning, I felt genuine fear. I know he saw it. I *hate* that he saw it. I hate that it hurt his feelings, and I know it did. But the emotion was instinctive, there before I could call it back. I'm not afraid of him, not exactly. But I'd be lying if I said I weren't afraid.

He says his club is different. I want to believe him. I just.... Did Siobhan want to believe the same thing when Danny introduced her to his club? Did she think they were just a bunch of guys who enjoyed riding together? I don't know. I'm not my sister, and Tate isn't Danny, but trust has never come easy for me, especially when it comes to men.

I never knew my real dad, and my mom's boyfriends tended to be alcoholics and addicts with anger problems. She never let them hit me or Siobhan, but they roughed her up plenty. After growing up around them, dating has never high on my list of priorities.

Making up perfect men for the story apps I write is easy. Putting my faith in the real version is terrifying. I want to believe Tate when he says his club is nothing like the men who killed my sister, but what happens if I'm wrong? What happens to Scout if I'm wrong?

"Tate is a good guy," Troian says, sobering. "You know I wouldn't have left you there alone if I didn't trust him implicitly to take care of you and Scout."

"I know," I whisper, laying my forehead against the cool glass and exhaling a sigh. It immediately fogs over a patch of glass beneath my nose. Guilt trickles in, adding to the cacophony battling for dominion in my mind. She's right. "I feel like a jerk. He's been great, and I basically called him a criminal today."

"He'll forgive you. Besides, a little humility will do him good," she says with a chuckle. "He's cocky, isn't he?"

"He's bossy."

"That too." She laughs. "Give him a chance, Samara. He's an incredible surgeon, and a good man. He'll be good for you and Scout."

I frown, not sure I like the way she said that. "You mean for Scout."

"Sure, that," she says. "How is she today?"

"Worse," I whisper, tears pooling in my eyes. Every day, she's worse than the day before. I hate leaving because I'm so afraid something will happen while I'm gone. Her heart is struggling. Her lungs are struggling. *She's* struggling. They keep telling me that she's a fighter, but she shouldn't have to fight at all. No baby should.

"I'm so sorry, Samara."

"Me too."

"Do you have a surgery date yet?"

"Tate's working on it." He left her room to start making calls not long after Daisy, her nurse, arrived. He still hadn't returned by the time visiting hours ended. I decided to walk back to the penthouse to clear my head. Hopefully he'll have a date for me soon. "I'm not sure how much time he needs."

"If anyone can get it worked out for her, he can. She's in good hands now." She pauses. "That's what they call him, you know. Hands."

"Really?"

"Mmhmm."

An image of him running his hands across my body floats through my mind, his emerald eyes locked on my face. A shiver rolls through me. I bite my lip, fighting a groan.

Stop thinking about his hands, Samara. Stop thinking about him.

Except...I can't. All day, he's been stuck in my head. It's starting to stress me out. The walk here didn't help. Nothing has. Ever since this morning, I've been obsessing about him, and I don't know why. He's not the first gorgeous man I've met. There are plenty of those in California. But he's the first one that I've ever wanted to know.

"I should go," I say. "I need to shower and get some sleep."

"Call me if you need anything, Samara. I mean it," Troian orders, her voice soft. "I'll be on the first flight out."

"Thank you," I whisper, fighting tears again. I have no idea how I would have made it through the last few years without her and her family. Troian didn't just give me a job. When she hired me to work at her family's company, they adopted me. Her parents, Dom and Summer, treat me like one of their kids. Without them, I'd be entirely on my own.

Once we say our goodbyes, I pull my charger out of my bag and plug it in to charge my phone. I don't have much with me, but Tate helped me carry it up before we went to the hospital earlier. As soon as my phone is charging, I grab clothes and head toward the bathroom for a long, hot shower.

It's the only room in the apartment not completely made of glass. On a good day, this bathroom is a luxury. After spending the last week showering in the hospital shower, it's pure bliss. The floors are heated. Hot water pours from three different shower heads. I use more than my fair share of the hot water, letting it beat down on me. For once, my mind is quiet. I think I'm too tired to worry and cry and stress anymore today.

I barely have my t-shirt and panties on when the bathroom door flies open, banging against the wall. I jump a foot into the air, my hand flying to my heart.

"You left," Tate growls, glaring at me like a pissed off lion.

"You scared the crap out of me!"

"You left," he says again.

"Visiting hours ended." My stomach sinks, anxiety shooting through me. "Did something happen? Is Scout okay?"

"She's fine, angel." He grabs me around the waist, hauling me up against his hard body before I can rush past him. "Nothing has changed."

I sag in his arms, relief loosening my muscles all at once. "I thought..."

"I'm an idiot." His palm settles against my abdomen, his nose sliding down the side of my face. "I scared you."

"Every time I leave, I worry something is going to happen," I admit, melting deeper into his embrace. I tell myself it's just for a minute. That I'll pull away again when my legs stop trembling. But I think I'm lying to myself. It's been so damn long since anyone held me. His arms feel like heaven around me.

"I'm not going to let anything happen to her, baby. I made you a promise. I don't intend to break it now." His lips track down my cheek, his words a soft murmur against my skin.

Even though I shouldn't, I tilt my head, allowing him access to my throat. His stubble scrapes my skin in the most wicked, delicious way as he attacks my neck with his lips and tongue. His hand tightens on my stomach, pulling me closer. His—oh, lord—his erection digs into the small of my back.

"Why'd you leave?" he growls against my skin.

"V-visiting hours."

"Don't apply to you, Samara. We both know it. Why'd you leave?"

He's right. They don't. I can come and go whenever I want. Parents and caregivers have access to the hospital twenty-four hours a day, seven days a week. It's the saddest perk of having a child in intensive care, one no one ever wants to have to utilize and yet we find ourselves intensely grateful to have anyway.

"I don't know," I whisper.

"You're afraid."

I nod miserably.

He stops kissing my neck and turns me to face him. One gentle finger beneath my chin angles my head back until my gaze tangles with his. I get lost in those dark emerald eyes again, in the emotion swirling through their depths. Yes, this man is bossy. Maybe even cocky and arrogant, but there's so much more to him too.

"Are you afraid of me, Samara?"

Am I? I give the question the consideration it deserves. He may be in a motorcycle club. That fact may scare the crap out of me. But I'm not afraid of *him*. Even now, knowing the truth, I feel safer with him than I've ever felt with anyone.

"No," I confess on a whisper. "I'm not afraid of you."

His pleased smile is pure sin. It sends a bolt of white-hot desire racing through my veins, liquefying them on contact.

"Good girl," he rumbles, tipping his head down toward mine. "I'll never hurt you, Samara. I'd fucking annihilate anyone who tried."

"I..." I lick my lips, not sure *thanks* is the proper response to such a statement.

"You and Scout are mine now, angel. I protect what's mine."

"W-what's yours? We're not property, Tate."

"Never said you were. You don't worship property," he murmurs, brushing his nose against mine. "You don't adore and covet and spoil it. I plan to do all those things for you and Scout. And when she's tucked away in her bed at night, sleeping peacefully, I intend to do it all over again just for you."

Oh, lord.

"I'm going to worship you on my knees with my tongue tucked between your thighs, Samara," he growls. "I'm going to spoil you with these hands, this mouth, and this dick."

"Tate," I groan, my head spinning. Is it normal for doctors to talk this way? Surely it isn't. Gage doesn't say these things, not around me anyway. And yet...and yet they sound perfectly right coming from Tate's wicked lips. There isn't another doctor like him in the world, I'm sure of it.

"I'm going to give you the world, angel. As soon as you let me in."

Let him in? I'm pretty sure he knows more about me in one day than Troian learned the whole first year we knew each other. Opening up doesn't come naturally to me. My life has never been easy. It's never been pretty. If I don't count on anyone or get close to anyone, it hurts less when they inevitably disappear from my life.

"Kiss me," he orders, rubbing his nose against mine. "I need one little taste to hold me over."

I should tell him no, but I don't. He's in my personal space, working sex magic on my senses. I close the sliver of space between us, eagerly pressing my lips to his. For a protracted second, time seems to stand still. Neither of us move as electricity courses through me in a powerful deluge.

And then he grunts and I'm in his arms, my legs around his waist. His tongue thrusts into my mouth as his hands slip into the back of my panties, grabbing two handfuls of my ass. He grinds me against his erection, snarling like a starving lion.

I make the same desperate, needy sound, yanking on his hair, trying to get closer to him. Reality spirals away, leaving nothing but want and need and *take*. It's primal, elemental, and somehow sexy as hell too. There's something so raw about it, so unrefined. This isn't some carefully planned seduction. This is desire in its purest form. It's *us*, sparking like kindling and going up in flames.

"Fuck yeah," he groans, biting my lip. "Rub that pretty cunt all over me, angel."

I do. God help me, I do. I can't stop myself.

We stumble out of the bathroom and into the bedroom, locked together like two connected puzzle pieces. Halfway to the bed, I realize the ringing in my ears isn't blood pumping through my system. It's his phone.

"Tate," I gasp.

"Say my name again," he growls. "Louder."

"Tate, wait. Your phone."

For a minute, I think he's going to ignore me, but he growls a curse and reluctantly fishes it out of his pocket.

"What?" he snaps, his eyes blazing with deadly heat as they track across my face. Oh my. He does not like being interrupted.

I can't hear whoever he's talking to, but whatever they say instantly snaps him into focus. The haze clears between one heartbeat and the next as he carefully tucks the wild man away and slips into surgeon mode.

"When?" he asks and then listens for a minute. "Call Dr. Davidson in from pulmonary and prep the OR. I'll be there in fifteen minutes."

For the second time in twenty minutes, my heart stops beating for a second before leaping ahead with a jarring thud. Tate notices. As soon as he disconnects, he tosses the phone onto the bed, wrapping both arms around me.

"It's not Scout," he says. "Breathe, baby."

I suck in a deep breath, letting it out on a shaky exhale. "I thought..."

"I know." He rubs my back. "It's not her. It's not going to be her." He carries me to the bed and sits down with me in his lap. "Look at me."

I tilt my head back, meeting his gaze.

"We're performing her surgery first thing on Thursday morning," he says, his voice soft. "She'll be in the OR before the sun rises."

"Thursday?" I whisper, stunned. That's only three days from now. I don't know why, but I thought it would take longer. I guess I assumed it would take weeks to iron out the details, not days. She was in such bad shape when she got here, I think most of the other doctors never expected her to make it to surgery. They certainly haven't been in a rush to get her into the OR, which is exactly why Gage called Tate. Honestly, I think they're afraid to operate on her. They gave up on her before they even gave her a chance. Not Tate.

"Thursday." Tate cups my cheek in his palm. "It can't wait, angel. She's getting weaker by the day. The longer we wait, the riskier it gets. That's not a risk I'm willing to take with her or you. We've got to get in there now."

I bob my head in understanding, tears of gratitude welling in my eyes. No, I'm not afraid of this man. How can I be? He's fought harder for my niece in one day than anyone else has all week. I barely know him, but in this moment, a little piece of my heart falls into his hands.

I lean forward and press my lips to his before quickly pulling back.

"Thank you," I whisper, roughly clearing my throat. "For fighting for her."

He thumbs my tears away, bumping his forehead against mine. "You should know, I'm not just fighting for Scout. I'm fighting for you too. As soon as she's out of the woods, I'm going to make you fall in love with me, Samara Lansing."

I don't tell him that I think I might already be falling.

"You can't boss me into falling for you, Tate," I say instead, rolling my eyes.

"I'm not going to boss you." He picks me up again, smirking. "I'm going to spoil you with this dick until you forget other men exist. But keep rolling those eyes at me and I'll be spanking that pretty ass as soon as I finish this surgery."

"I will smother you with a pillow."

"No, you won't." He carries me to the head of the bed and pulls the covers back before depositing me beneath them. "Then you won't have anyone to cuddle with tonight." He drops a kiss on my forehead before pulling the covers up over me. "Rest, Sleeping Beauty. I'll be back as soon as I can."

"You're sleeping on the couch," I mumble, burrowing into the blankets.

"Uh, fuck no," he growls. "I'm sleeping with one hand on my pussy, and the other over one of those sexy tits. You can be mad about it tomorrow."

His pussy? Oh, lord. Why is that so sexy?

"Dream of me, Sleeping Beauty," he orders on his way out the door.

"Good luck, Tate," I whisper.

"Keep wiggling like that and you'll be finishing what you started last night, angel," Tate drawls from behind me, his voice gritty from sleep.

I freeze mid-wiggle, my stomach clenching.

His soft chuckle sends pieces of hair dancing along my neck. My skin turns to gooseflesh, my core igniting. God, he sounds even better when he first wakes up than he does the rest of the time, which is saying something because the man sounds like he could run his own phone-sex line.

His hand around my waist tightens, dragging me back toward him.

"You snore," he murmurs, nuzzling his face into the back of my neck.

"I do not," I gasp.

"You do. It's the cutest sound I've ever heard."

"I do not snore."

"You talk too."

"Do not," I whisper, praying I didn't say anything horribly embarrassing.

"What, exactly, is sex on legs?" he asks, sending that hope up in a puff of smoke.

"I don't know what you're talking about," I sniff, deciding to play ignorant instead of answering that question. Maybe if I don't encourage him, he won't tell me what I said and I can live in blissful ignorance for the rest of my life. It's better than squirming in shame for the rest of eternity. "I don't talk in my sleep, and I've never heard that saying before in my life."

"Liar," he says, his deep chuckle vibrating against my back. "I bet next you're going to tell me you weren't moaning my name and begging me to kiss you."

I gasp and flip over to face him. "I was not!"

His cocky smirk says it all. I was moaning his name in my sleep. And begging him to kiss me. Oh my gosh. I should have slept on the couch! But as soon as he turned out the light, I was asleep. I never even heard him come in last night.

"You're evil and I don't like you," I mutter, glaring at him.

"You seemed to like me just fine when you were—"

I slap my hand over his mouth, silencing him.

He laughs quietly, his sleepy eyes tracking across my face. How it's possible for him to be even more attractive in the morning, I don't know, but he is. There's just something...delicious about seeing him all rumpled and messy. This is a side of him not many get to see, I think. The real him, not the one hidden behind his lab coat and confident smiles.

"How did your surgery go?" I ask, tracing the shadows beneath his eyes with my fingertips.

"Good," he says. "My patient is going to be fine."

"That's good," I whisper, relieved. "Can I ask you a question?"

"Sure."

"Why pediatrics?"

"I played football as a kid," he says, watching me intently. "My best friend was on my team. He collapsed during a game one day. He had a heart condition no one knew about." A shadow passes through his eyes. "He was nine years old and went into cardiac arrest."

"Oh, Tate," I whisper. "Did he—?"

"They were able to save him," he says. "But he had to give up sports, live life on the sidelines for most of his childhood. I decided then that I wanted to be the guy who kept other kids from going through that, so that's what I did."

"That's really sweet," I murmur. "Are you still friends?"

"We are." He smiles at me. "Kaiden works in the film industry. Believe it or not, he's a former stunt-man."

"Seriously?" I gape at him. "He was a stuntman with a heart condition?"

"He was," he confirms, amusement lighting his eyes. "He retired after he was injured during a stunt. Now, he does a lot of stunt coordinating and train-ing." He runs his hand up my thigh, sending a shiver through me. "What do you do, angel? You work for Troian?"

"I write choose your own adventure romance games for the app-development side of her family's tech company," I murmur, watching him through my lashes as he plays with the hem of my t-shirt. "I've been with them since they bought my first game." She didn't even bat a lash at the fact that I was still in college. As soon as she played through the game, she and her dad hired me on the spot.

"Choose your own adventure romance?" He quirks a brow at me. "What the fuck is that?"

"It's exactly what it sounds like. I write a bunch of different storylines and outcomes, and then users decide what happens at various stages of the game. Do they go home with the hot firefighter or go home alone? Do they flirt with the single dad next door or slam the door in his face?" I explain, smiling. "They're a lot of fun to write."

"Are they dirty?"

"Sometimes."

He grins at me, waggling his brows suggestively. "How dirty?"

He would want to know that.

"Well," I say, pretending to think about my answer. "I used to be involved in this secret club in San Diego. It was by invitation only. Some filthy things happened there. Like this one time, four different men took–"

I squeal when I land on my back with him on top of me.

"If that sentence ends with them doing anything to you, don't even think about finishing it," he growls, his eyes flashing holy fire at me. "And I need to know the name of this fucking club so I can burn it to the ground."

"I was just kidding, Tate," I say, caught off guard by the intensity in his gaze. I didn't intend to make him jealous, only to tease him back a little. "There was no club or four men. There were no men, for that matter. I'm, um..." I squirm.

"Say it," he growls.

"I'm a virgin," I whisper.

"Not for long," he says, slipping a hand between us to cup my sex. He grips it in his palm, his touch possessive. "This part of you is mine, Samara. No one sees it. No one touches it. No one eats it or fucks it but me."

"Tate," I moan, my body going limp beneath him.

He grinds his thumb against my clit, finding it with startling accuracy. "No one touches me either, Samara. Once I'm in you, it's permanent. There will be no one else for either of us. God, I can feel how wet you are for me." He grinds his thumb against my clit again. Even through my panties, I hear the wet sounds of my sex. I know he can too.

"Tate, I...I..."

"You're going to come for me, aren't you?"

I nod, trying to fight it off, but I can't. It's too big, too powerful.

"Do it, angel. Let me watch it take you," he breathes, eyes locked on my face as he slips my panties to the side and parts my slit with his bare thumb.

As soon as I feel his skin against mine, it's over for me. A detonation sparks in my lower belly, setting off a chain reaction. *Pow. Pow. Pow pow pow.* I cry out his name, my back arching off the bed as waves of bliss crest and then crash down over me. They fling me this way and that, leaving me wrung out and trembling.

"Beautiful," Tate whispers, capturing my lips with his. He kisses me hard and deep, his hand still between my legs. I cling to him, shaking as aftershocks work their way through me. He strokes me through them, gently bringing me back down.

I land in his arms, feeling better than I have since the police showed up to inform me about Siobhan. No, that's not right. I feel better than I have in...ever.

He kisses me until I stop shaking and then gently slips his hand from between my legs.

I hide my face in the pillow when he pops his fingers into his mouth to lick them clean. He chuckles, pulling me into his arms.

"I love how shy you are," he murmurs, running a soothing hand down my back.

"I'm not shy."

"You are."

"Am not. You're just cocky."

He smirks at me.

I ignore him.

"I have to head back to Silver Spoon Falls today, angel."

"Oh," I whisper, swallowing hard. Not sure what to say. Thanks for the orgasm, see you later? I'm not sure what to do here, but I suddenly feel awkward and out of my depth. "Um..."

"I can hear you thinking all the way over here," he drawls.

"Are you...glad?"

"Am I glad that I'm leaving you here alone? Fuck no," he says, narrowing his eyes at me. "I'd rather spend the day at Scout's bedside with you, bring you back here tonight, and fuck you to sleep. I know it's the only way you'll actually sleep. But I have patients scheduled this afternoon and then an MC thing this evening."

"Oh." I exhale a breath, relieved he's not leaving because he doesn't want to be here with me. "Sorry," I whisper. "Um...people in my life tend not to stick around for long."

"Then they aren't worthy of being in your life," he says, tipping my head back to press his lips to mine. "I'm not going anywhere, Samara." He grimaces.

"I'm going to Silver Spoon Falls today, but I mean, long term, I'm here. We're doing this. I know you don't know me well enough yet to trust me, but give me time. That's all I'm asking for right now."

"Okay," I whisper, willing to give him that.

"Actually, I lied." He grimaces again. "I'm asking for something else too."

"What?" I ask, suspicious.

"I want you to give my brothers a chance," he says, his voice soft. "I want you to meet them, see for yourself that they aren't like the men who killed your sister."

I exhale a deep breath, reaching deep for a little courage. If he's asking for this, I think I owe it to him to try. Even if we end in disaster, I still owe him this much. These guys are important to him and right now, he thinks I hate them.

"Okay," I agree, clinging to courage with both hands. "I'll meet them."

"Yeah?" he asks.

"Yeah."

His blinding smile makes me feel like a lion.

CHAPTER FIVE

Tate

"What crawled up your ass?" Andreas "Playboy" Romano asks, eyeing me over the rim of his glass, one dark brow arched in question. "You've been in a mood all night."

"Nothing," I lie, shaking my head.

We both know I'm full of shit, but Playboy doesn't press me on it. He just grunts and goes back to his thousand-dollar brandy, content to wait me out.

Unlike a lot of our brothers, Playboy tends to be on the quiet side. He's dealt with his fair share of drama, thanks to the shady dealings of his late father. Vincent knew how to make a scene. Playboy is different. He's playing chess while everyone else is playing checkers. Fifth likes to think we're some of the smartest men in the club. He's wrong. Playboy has us all beat by miles. He's just smart enough to keep his mouth shut. The man is a viper, striking from the shadows.

I pull my phone out and check it for the thousandth time tonight. Samara still hasn't responded to my last message. I'm guessing she's still at Scout's bedside. She's texted me a few times today, but not often. Every time I called the hospital to check on Scout, she was at her side. I hate that she's there alone while I'm at the compound like this is any other night. But driving back to Houston tonight isn't an option when I have to be back here first thing in the morning.

It's pissing me off. My girls have spent far too much time alone already.

My girls. Fuck, I like the sound of that.

I lift my head, looking for Cash. He's on the far side of the bar with Hadley, his hand splayed across her belly. I catch his eye and motion him over. He lifts his chin in a nod and then murmurs something to his girl before he kisses her and heads my way, a beer in hand.

Fifth spots him headed in my direction and excuses himself from a conversation with Hacker. He meets Cash halfway. They stroll toward me and Playboy, crossing the bar quickly. Except for Fifth's olive skin, they could almost pass for biological brothers. They're both big, with dark hair and darker eyes.

Several of our brothers watch them moving in our direction but no one else follows. They turn back to their conversations, giving us privacy. They all know something is up though. I was distracted all throughout Church. That's unusual for me and they all know it.

"What's up, brother?" Cash asks, claiming the empty stool to my right.

Fifth opts to stand near Playboy instead of taking a barstool.

"I'm not going to be around much for a while," I say. "I've got some shit going on in Houston."

"A patient?" Cash asks.

"A girl," Fifth says, smirking.

Bastard.

I narrow my eyes on him. He flips me off in return, taking a pull from his bottle.

"That's why you're in a bad mood?" Playboy laughs. "Shit. I thought you lost a patient or something the way you've been acting all night. I was preparing myself for the fact that none of us were sleeping tonight until you were thoroughly wasted. Instead, you're fucked up over a girl."

"Karma's a bitch," Fifth says.

Playboy laughs.

"Man, fuck both of you," I growl. "I'm not in a bad mood. I had an emergency surgery in the middle of the night."

"Mmhmm," Fifth says, smirking.

I turn to Cash, only to find him smirking at me too. Of course he's loving this too. My friends are all assholes.

"It's not just a girl," I say, shaking my head. "Her niece has a congenital heart defect. I'm operating first thing Thursday morning. I need to be there in case anything goes wrong."

"Of course," Cash says, his smirk slipping as his expression grows serious. "What do you need?"

"For someone else to deal with Brady," I mutter. Sheriff Armstrong was at the office today to discuss him. Jules had to agree to a date to get him to leave.

"I'll put someone on it," Cash promises.

"Can we do anything?" Playboy asks, as serious as Cash. We may give each other hell, but this is what the brotherhood is about. We're family. No one ever fights alone, no matter the battle. It doesn't matter if they've met Samara and Scout or not. If they're mine, they're family. Every man in this club knows what that means.

"I'd like to bring Samara to meet everyone," I say, turning slightly to include him and Fifth in this conversation. "But she has...issues with motorcycle clubs." I cut my eyes at Fifth. "One murdered her sister."

"Fuck," Cash growls, his dark brows slashing together.

"Satan's Savages," Fifth supplies, letting me know he's already done some digging for me.

I jerk my chin in a nod, silently giving him permission to tell us what he knows.

"They ran her off the road right outside of the police station in Dallas," he says, speaking quietly. "It looks like she was on her way there but her old man and two other members got to her first. They holed up in a bakery across the street after the accident. Her old man decided to shoot his way out once he realized he wasn't going to walk out a free man. Got himself killed too."

Jesus. I knew Samara wasn't joking when she told me they killed her sister, but Jesus.

"The sister lived long enough to tell them about the baby," Fifth says, looking at me. "I guess she hid the baby in a bathroom somewhere along the way to keep her safe. She asked them to save her baby and to call her sister."

"Jesus," Cash whispers, grim fury burning in his eyes. Hadley was in a car accident not long ago. He knows exactly what it's like to worry about losing a kid. He'll never admit it, but he still worries. "That's fucked."

"Beyond," Playboy agrees, his mouth set in a hard, unforgiving line.

"They found a note with the baby," Fifth says. "Apparently, the sister found out her old man was trafficking women for the MC and helped several of them escape. Once the MC found out, they locked her up to keep her from going to the authorities."

"Did she implicate anyone else from the MC in the trafficking scheme?" I ask.

"Don't know," Fifth says, shaking his head. "Dallas PD was tight-lipped on that. All they'd say was that they were looking into the allegations against the MC."

"No wonder the sister is gun shy about MCs," Cash muses, running a hand down his chin. "Can't say I blame her." He casts a glance around the clubhouse. The two-story white, plantation-style compound looks more like a home than anything. The bar where we're sitting stretches across the back wall, with tables scattered around the room. Two pool tables take up the center of the room. Hacker rigged up an old jukebox to a computer and a sound system. It plays anything we want. The speakers are hidden in alcoves along the top of the wall, allowing music to spill out into the room.

Unlike a lot of MC compounds, this one isn't filled with women. Aside from Gloria and Hadley, not many come through here. Most of our brothers don't fuck around. Those who do tend to keep that shit out of the club. This place is a second home to most of us. We come here to relax and let loose without prying eyes. But there's still no mistaking that it's an MC compound.

Replicas of bikes hang on the walls alongside our emblem. The furniture is dark wood and worn leather. Harsh lighting gives it a club glow. Not even Gloria's immaculate housekeeping softens the masculine vibe to the place. Bringing Samara here isn't likely to ease her into anything.

"Her niece's surgery is Thursday morning?" Cash asks.

"Yeah, first thing."

"We'll be there," he says. "As many of us as can be, anyway. Bender's still on tour."

"Shit. You don't have to do that."

"You plan on putting a patch on her?" he asks, cocking a brow at me.

I jerk my chin in a nod. Maybe it's too soon to be thinking about shit like getting my patch on her or my ring on her finger but that ship sailed about the time she kissed me last night. Hell, I think it sailed about the time I saw her yesterday morning. I'm not going to fight it or deny it.

"Then we're doing it," Cash says, pointing his bottle at me. "She shouldn't have to go through this shit alone anyway. We'll keep her company while you put that Ivy League education to work."

I clasp him on the shoulder, grateful as hell. "Thank you."

"Don't thank me. She hasn't met these fuckers yet," he says, smacking me on the back. He chuckles and then heads back across the room toward Hadley.

Fifth gives Playboy a nod, silently telling him to give us a minute. Playboy empties his glass and then rises to his feet without a word. He takes off in the opposite direction from Cash, straightening his suit as he goes.

"You have something else for me?" I ask Fifth.

"Depends," he says, taking the stool Playboy just vacated. He wraps his fingers around his bottle, toying with it. "How much do you want to know about your girl?"

"Only what you think I need to know to protect her," I say. Anything beyond that, I want to hear from her lips. Her story is hers to tell. I appreciate Fifth for digging, but I'm not interested in what he found. I doubt she'd appreciate knowing I heard it from him either.

"Keep her close," he warns me. "The Savages are dangerous, and your girl is worth money. She's made a small fortune for herself in the gaming market. I highly doubt they'll come after her and the baby but keep her close just in case."

"Thanks, brother," I say, appreciative as hell. If the Savages think they're coming after her, they better think again. We don't have to break the law to be a problem. Every man in this MC can bury them without spilling a drop of blood. We have the type of connections they lose sleep thinking about at night...federal agents, the secret service, Supreme Court Justices, royalty.

I don't think they'll be a problem though. At least not for Samara. If they were hanging on to Siobhan because she was pregnant, they were doing it for Scout's father. With him dead, Scout means nothing to any of them. There's no reason for them to come after her or Samara.

I'll still be keeping them close though.

"Fill Cash in, will you?" I ask Fifth, climbing to my feet.

"Will do," he agrees.

I pause, turning back to him. "Did you look up any of her games?"

He jerks his chin in a nod.

"Text me the names of them, will you?"

A wolfish grin crosses his face.

I pretend not to see it. Nosy bastard.

"You've been naughty."

"Ahh!" Samara shouts, flinging her phone into the air.

I chuckle, watching as her hand flies to her heart, and she ducks, dodging her phone as it drops back down, landing at her feet with a thunk.

"Stop doing that!" she yells, slamming her hands down on her hips to glare at me. She looks angelic with her dark hair up in a messy bun, wispy pieces floating freely around her heart-shaped face. "Jesus, Tate!" And then she seems to realize that I'm actually here instead of in Silver Spoon Falls where I'm supposed to be. Her eyes light up as they prowl across my bare chest, her irritated expression softening. "You're here."

"I am," I say, tossing my phone on the bedside table and then jack-knifing up from the bed. I prowl across the room toward her, my cock turning to steel the closer I get. "Did you miss me?"

"What are you doing here?" She cranes her head back to look at me.

"I decided I like this bed more than my other bed," I mutter, reaching out to tap her nose. Truth is, I intended to go to my place in Silver Spoon Falls when I left the clubhouse...but I didn't. I drove straight here instead, breaking every speed limit along the way. The thought of letting her sleep alone tonight didn't appeal to me. I'll wake up early in the morning and make the drive back. Seeing the softness in her eyes right now is more than worth the lack of sleep.

"I think you like the girl sharing this bed," she says, her mouth curving into a sweet smile.

"Oh, I definitely like the girl sharing this bed," I growl, pulling her into my arms. "Especially when she's moaning my name in her sleep. *Tate. Tate. Oh, Tate.*"

"I do not sound like that."

"You do," I whisper, pressing my mouth to hers.

"Do not."

"Less arguing, more kissing."

"Bossy."

She kisses me when I growl, her soft lips melting against mine. Fuck, she tastes like those hard candies my mom used to keep in her purse for her models. She said it made them less irritable when a shoot ran long. Xavier and I stole them constantly. They were sweet and tangy. Samara's mouth is more addictive than they were.

I stroke her tongue with mine until we're both panting and then reluctantly break away. She sways in my arms, her cheeks flushed pink. Her lashes flutter, her gold eyes opening. They're soft and warm, full of liquid desire.

"You were at the hospital late," I murmur, thrusting my hand into her hair. I gently grab a handful, pulling slightly. Her eyes gloss over, her lips parting. "Is everything okay?"

"F-fine," she says. "I was just visiting with Scout."

"Yeah?" I smile, leaning down to kiss her hot little mouth again. "Did you have a good visit, angel?"

"They let me hold her," she whispers.

"Yeah?"

She nods. "They haven't let me do that before."

"I know." I run my nose along the side of hers, placing a trail of kisses along her cheek. Dr. Shapiro is old school when it comes to medicine. If it were up to him, kids in PICU would heal in glass bubbles with their families firmly on the outside, watching from a safe distance. There is no convincing him of the power of human touch, regardless of how many studies you wave in his face. I disagree with him entirely.

Kids, especially babies, thrive on comfort and care. They need to be held and loved. Samara should have been allowed to hold Scout long before now, so I remedied the situation. Until the surgery, she'll be allowed to hold her for an hour or two at a time every day. After surgery, it'll be a while before she's able to hold her again. I want her to have this time to bond with her now, while she's able. She deserves that much.

"You did that?" she whispers, awe in her voice.

"I just signed the order."

"Thank you." She places her hand on my cheek, her eyes meeting mine. Gratitude burns golden in their depths. "Thank you."

"Did it help?"

"So much," she whispers, blinking rapidly. "She's so tiny and sweet. I didn't want to leave."

"She's not the only sweet one."

"I love her so much, Tate," she says.

"She's going to love you back the same way."

"You think so?" she asks, worrying her bottom lip.

"I know so." I grin, not surprised that's her fear. She hasn't shown a single ounce of fear about stepping up for this fragile baby. She hasn't balked at caring for her or providing for her or becoming a caregiver at the age of twenty-two. Already, she loves Scout with her whole heart and soul. Her only concern is whether Scout will love her too. It's as fucking adorable as it is sad that she doesn't know how infinitely lovable she is. "I'm a doctor. I basically know everything."

"You are so full of it," she laughs, shaking her head at me.

"Maybe, but in this case, I'm right." Scout will adore her. I know this for a fact because I already adore her. She's too goddamn sweet not to love on sight. Shit. Is that what's happening here? Of course it is. I'm falling for her. *Hard*. I gave Cash so much shit for falling for Hadley at the speed of light, but I think I may be beating his record over here. Samara's already burrowing her way into my soul, claiming parts of it I didn't even know existed.

Every time she smiles at me, another piece of it falls to her light. Every time she laughs, another section hoists her colors. Soon enough, every square inch will belong to her. My MC brothers think I've been running from love my whole life but that's not true. I've been waiting for the right kind of love to find me. *This* kind. The kind that knocked my dad on his ass the day he met my mom. The kind that took my Uncle Gray out when he met my Aunt Camilla. The men in my family fall hard, holding nothing back.

If I was meant to have it, I figured it'd find me like it did them. I wasn't wrong. Fate brought Samara into my life. Cash would call it karma for all the bitching I did. He'd be wrong. This right here, this is divine providence. And I can't fucking wait to belong to this delicate little angel with the warrior's soul. I was never running from love. I was waiting for *her*.

"I've been busy while you were gone," I murmur, reaching down to scoop her phone up off the floor. I hold it out to her, smiling when she shoves it into her pocket without even finishing whatever she was doing when she walked in.

"Texting me doesn't count as busy, Tate," she sasses. "I don't see how you got anything done all day. You sent me like nine hundred messages today."

"I did not send you that many texts." I probably did send her that many texts, but that's beside the point. "What I was talking about, smartass, was this fascinating new game I've been playing while waiting for you to get home from visiting Scout."

"What game?" Suspicion furrows her brows, narrowing her golden eyes.

"Like I said when you came in, you've been naughty," I growl, running my palm across her round ass. "One curvy human and an entire pack of shifters?"

"Oh. That game." Her cheeks heat, turning the sweetest pink.

"Yeah, *that* game."

She practically squirms on her feet.

"Did it get you hot, thinking about being taken by five men at once like that, Samara?"

"No," she says, scrunching up her nose. "But other women like it. You shouldn't kink shame. It's not nice, Tate."

Kink shame? Hell. I'll give this dirty little angel whatever she wants so long as it doesn't involve another man. Any fantasy she has, I'll bring to life. "I haven't blushed since I was a kid, Sleeping Beauty," I say, nipping at her ear. "Your little game changed that."

"Then you definitely don't want to hear about the VR version Troian wants to develop," she says, humor in her voice. "It'll have you clutching your pearls."

"You're not playing with VR cocks, Samara," I growl. Hell no. The only cock she's touching is mine. I don't care if they're imaginary or not. It's not happening. Just playing the damn game had me ready to spank her for writing it.

"I'm not playing with any cocks," she says.

I hear the pout in her voice even though she tries to hide it. My sweet angel is horny. And curious. Fuck. Where has she been all my life?

"Put your hands in my pants, Samara," I order her. "Take my dick out."

"Tate," she moans.

"Now, angel."

She places her palm on my abdomen and then slides it downward. My muscles contract beneath her hand, responding to her touch. God, she has no idea how good that feels. Her fingers slip beneath the waistband of my sweats, the tip of her tongue peeking from between her lips as if she's concentrating hard on her task.

I growl when she runs her knuckles across the swollen head of my cock. Cum spills across her fingers, making her gasp. Her gaze flies to mine.

"Yeah, baby," I say through a chuckle. "He's happy to see you."

"Did you just...?"

"Not yet. I'm going to do that in your sweet mouth. Take him out," I say.

She doesn't slap me or tell me to go to hell, which I take as a good sign. Her tongue swiping across her bottom lip like she trying to taste me on it seems like another good sign.

She wraps her hand around my cock, her grip loose.

"Tighter. You won't hurt me. I like it rough."

"Of course you do," she mutters, rolling her eyes.

I swat her ass, which makes her squeak indignantly. "I warned you about rolling your eyes at me, Samara."

Fire flashes in her gaze, her grip tightening on my dick. My little angel turns into a curvy devil between one heartbeat and the next. She twists her wrist, stroking her hand down my length all the way to my balls.

"Fuck," I groan, trying not to lose it right there.

"Is this rough enough, *Doctor* Grimes?" She does it again, stroking upward this time. I don't know where the fuck she learned to do that and I'm not about to ask. If it was from some other man, I will lose my goddamn mind. The thought of her with anyone else drives me crazy. Reading her story had possessiveness churning through me. It makes no sense. It's fiction, purely a figment of her imagination. But it pissed me off, nonetheless.

Is this what Cash meant when he said Hadley turned him into a territorial beast? If so, he wasn't kidding. I don't want to share even a single part of Samara. If she's not thinking about me when she's touching herself, she's not touching herself. I'll be the name she says when she gets herself off from now on. I intend to make sure of it.

"Keep calling me that and we'll see how loud you can scream my name with my dick down your throat, Samara," I growl, wrapping my hand up in her hair again. I crane her head back, pulling gently. She loves it. Her eyes go glassy, her lips parting on a moan. "I suggest you behave before we're doing a whole lot of shit you aren't ready to do yet."

"Who says I'm not ready?" she challenges.

"I do." I press a hard kiss to her mouth. "You aren't ready for me yet, angel. Not until you're ready to give me this part of you too." I place my free hand between her breasts, splaying it over her heart. "Until then, I'm not taking that sweet little cherry."

She whimpers her disappointment, shaking my resolve.

"Shh," I whisper, flicking my tongue against her lips. "I'm still going to take care of you, baby. While you're choking on my cock, I'm going to eat your pussy."

"Tate," she moans. Her hand goes slack around my cock.

"Stroke me, Samara." I deliver a little bite to her bottom lip.

She jolts back into action, squeezing me a little too hard. When I hiss, she immediately loosens her grip. Her thumb sweeps over the head in silent apology. Fuck, she's a natural at this. I already know when I get in her, it's going to be over for me. I'll be addicted. That's precisely why I need her on the same page before we take that step. If we're not and she gets spooked, it's going to rip my fucking heart out of my chest. I'll chase her, as far and as long as I have to chase her.

I'd rather not have to do it though. She and Scout belong here with me. I've been building this life for her for...shit, for most of my life, I think. I've been making her a home, gathering a tribe around me, one worthy of her. Now, she just has to let us love her.

She works my sweats down, freeing my cock.

"Tate," she whispers, her voice strangled.

"I played your game, Samara," I remind her. "Don't pretend you're shocked they come this big." She may be a virgin, but she's not a delicate little flower, that's for damn sure. She's a dirty little thing, with an imagination to rival even Giant's. God knows, he's a filthy bastard. "You'll be able to handle me just fine."

"I've never..."

I quirk a brow. "Not even a vibrator?"

She quickly shakes her head.

"Goddamn, angel," I growl, scooping her up in my arms to carry her to the bed before she has me coming all over myself instead of in that hot mouth. "You're not making him any softer."

"You're not making me any less nervous!" she cries.

"Trust me." I lay her out on the bed and then peel her shoes off, tossing them over my shoulder. "When the time comes, you'll be able to take me. But tonight, I don't want you thinking about that. Tonight is about making you feel good."

"I thought it was about making you feel good."

"Angel, eating that juicy cunt is going to make me feel like king of the earth," I say, completely serious. "Especially if you've got your mouth on my dick at the same time. Lift your hips."

She lifts her hips, allowing me to strip her pants down her legs.

I groan when I see her lacy pink boy shorts. They're indecent and innocent at the same time. They're already damp with her juices too, the seam soaked through. I can't wait to feel those thick thighs wrapped around my head while she's riding my face. I already know I'm going to have her seated on my tongue as often as humanly possible.

I lean down, kissing a trail up her leg. She startles and then relaxes with a soft sigh. Her legs part slightly, hips canted inward to hide her pussy from me. I can't get enough of how shy she is one minute and how sassy she is in the next. It's the sexiest combination.

The closer I get to her pussy, the more she shakes. My mouth waters, my stomach growling as her arousal grows stronger. She smells like heaven. I nip the soft skin of her thigh and then run my nose along the crease of her leg.

"Tate," she moans.

"Raise up." I help her sit up so I can strip her shirt and bra off her body, and then lay her back against the pillows. Fuck, she's gorgeous. There isn't a spot on her that isn't completely captivating, from the smattering of freckles across her chest to her hard pink nipples to the little lines across her belly. Her hourglass figure has my dick ready to break in half. My hands twitch, eager to sink into her wide hips while I'm pumping into her.

Her cheeks turn pink as I stare. She fidgets beneath me, digging her toes into the blankets. One hand creeps across her belly like she's trying to hide it from my gaze.

"Nu-uh." I grab her hand, shaking my head. "Don't hide from me, Samara."

"I just..." She huffs. "You're looking at me."

"I know."

"I mean *really* looking."

"I know."

She rolls her eyes. "It's weird."

I stand up and strip my pants the rest of the way off, kicking them away. Her gaze follows me, her eyes wide in her flushed face. Her tongue peeks out, swiping across her bottom lip as she looks me over, watching me just as intently as I watch her.

"Is it weird now, angel?" I ask, wrapping my fist around my cock.

She silently shakes her head.

"Looking at you gets me like this," I say, stroking my dick. "So you're just going to have to deal with me looking because I plan to do a whole hell of a lot of it. You're beautiful."

"So are you," she whispers shyly.

"Yeah?" I cock my head to the side, grinning. "You think so?"

"I do."

I crawl onto the bed with her again, leaning down to kiss her lips. I work my way down this time, stopping to lavish attention on her tits. They're full and high, fucking magnificent. She likes when I suck and bite her nipples. I leave love bites all over them, admiring every single little splotch that marks her as mine.

I'm not sure which of us is more worked up by the time I reach her pussy. She's writhing beneath me, whimpering my name in sweet little cries that have my dick leaking cum. I peel her panties from her body, tossing them off the side of the bed. I want to spread her out and eat her until she's screaming the roof down around us, but I already know if I get my mouth on her before she touches my dick, she won't be touching my dick. And she wanted to play.

"Come here," I say, settling my hands around her waist. I lift her to her knees and then lay back. "You're going to sit on my face, angel."

"I...Tate, I've never..."

"I know," I croon, running a hand down her side. I'm jealous over a fucking game she wrote, and my innocent angel has never even been touched. She's as pure as the driven snow. I can't wait to experience everything with this woman. "I've got you, Samara. Trust me."

She exhales a shaky breath and then nods.

I help guide her into place, chuckling when she hovers over my face like she's trying to levitate. "Baby, my mouth is about to become your new throne. I suggest you sit on it like you plan to stay a while," I growl, gripping her hips. She's so wet, she's damn near dripping onto my face already. If she doesn't sit soon, I'm not going to be responsible for what I do. "Sit, angel."

"You won't be able to breathe!" she cries.

"Did I say I wanted to breathe, or did I say I wanted to eat, Samara? Sit."

"Fine, but if you die, I better not go to jail," she huffs.

"Angel," I chuckle. "Sit your pretty ass down and get your mouth on my cock."

She tries to ease herself down little by little. After about two seconds, I've had about enough of that bullshit and pull her down onto my face. She cries out in shock...and then cries out again when I immediately attack her pussy like a starving man. She falls forward, her hands landing against my abdomen. As soon as her taste hits my system, I decide air isn't a necessity at all. This pussy though? I'll be living off it for the next seventy years. Minimum.

"Oh my God!" Samara cries. "Tate!"

"Get your mouth on my cock, Samara," I growl, yanking her down even lower.

She sobs my name and stretches forward. A moment later, her perfect hand wraps around my cock. I nearly come unglued when her tongue touches the head. She's timid at first, licking me like a lollipop, experimenting. I can tell by the way she stretches eagerly for more that she likes it. She's a greedy girl.

She teases me mercilessly, oblivious to exactly what she's doing to me as she explores. By the time she wraps those plump lips around the head of my cock, I'm in a race to get her off before I lose it down her throat. I'm clinging to control by the skin of my teeth. Every instinct I have screams at me to flip her over and pound into her until she's mine in every way, but I won't. I can't. I refuse to fuck this up by pushing her too far too fast.

I thrust my tongue into her little fuckhole, growling at how tight she is. At how wet she gets. God, where's she been all my life? I don't know. But I think I was supposed to meet her now. There's a reason I came into her life when I did, a reason she came into mine when she did. I don't believe in much, but I believe that. We're exactly where we're meant to be.

I pry her cheeks apart, pressing my thumb against her back entrance. She moans around my cock, tensing and relaxing as if she isn't sure if she likes it or not. That's all right though. She'll learn to love it. I toy with her, slowly getting her used to being touched there. She grinds against my face, riding it from above as her thighs tremble and shake around me. Whatever inhibitions she had about sitting on my face are long gone as she chases her orgasm.

I fuck her with my tongue, trying to hold off my own and get her there. It's close...damn close when she cups my balls in her hand and gently rolls them between her fingers. My hips arch off the bed, forcing more of my cock down her throat. She gags around my length.

I thrust my tongue deeper into her pussy, grinding my nose against her clit and jiggling my thumb against her asshole at the same time. She cries out around my cock, her body locking down around me.

She comes in a heated rush of liquid honey and throaty cries. Her juices drip down her thighs, soaking my face as she rocks and moans. Her thighs are clamped tight around my head, the walls of her pussy fluttering and pulsing against my tongue. It's the hottest thing I've ever experienced.

Feeling her coming all over me sets off my own orgasm. I try to lift her off, not sure she's ready for me to actually come down her throat, but she fights me like a little hellcat. Her nails dig into my thighs, her lips locked around my cock like she intends to stay there permanently. I give up trying to get her off and give her what she wants. My stomach clenches, cum shooting up my shaft.

I roar against her pussy, the world going black. Blood rushes in my ears in a torrent of sound. Everything slows, fading to this moment, to this woman. For one long moment, my world narrows to this...to *her*. And I realize that I was wrong earlier. I'm not falling for her. I hit the ground hours ago, leaving behind a crater miles wide.

This woman owns me.

Her and the fragile little girl waiting across the street for me to heal her heart.

CHAPTER SIX

Samara

"**S**amara."

I lift my gaze from Scout to see Carly standing beside my chair.

"Dr. Grimes is on his way up to see you," she says, smiling at me.

"Already?" I blink, glancing toward the television hanging over the bank of monitors beside Scout's bed. It's already after five. "I must have dozed off."

"You looked like you were sleeping peacefully," Carly says. "Miss Scout too." She nods at the baby still cuddled up on my chest, her head tucked carefully against my shoulder. "Her vitals haven't dropped once since you sat down with her."

"That's good," I say, exhaling a relieved breath. Her vitals have been all over the place today. Even though Tate was in Silver Spoon Falls most of the day, he's been checking in regularly. He had Carly turn Scout's oxygen up once because she was struggling so hard to breathe. I was beginning to worry it wasn't going to be enough, but her color looks better. I glance from her to the monitor, relaxing further when I see that her vitals are stronger.

"Do you need me to help you get her back in the bed?" Carly asks.

"I can do it," I say, waving her off. Now that I have permission to hold her, I find myself reluctant to share her with anyone. She's so tiny and cuddly. I love her so damn much already. It kills me that Siobhan isn't going to be here to see her grow up. I don't think I'll ever understand how my sister got involved with an MC like Danny's. But I'm no longer sure it matters. Regardless of what led her there, she made the right decision in the end. She tried to do the right thing. It cost her everything, but she died a hero.

Even if no one else ever knows her name or what she did, the women she saved will. Scout will. When she's old enough to hear the story, I'll tell her what her mom did to protect the women who needed it most. I don't know what I'll tell her about her dad. I haven't worked that part out yet. But she'll know her mom was a warrior. She'll know Siobhan did the right thing when it counted.

"You're so good with her," Carly says, watching as I rise carefully to my feet to place Scout back in her crib. I make sure all of her cords and wires are tucked out of the way and aren't pulling and then place her little blanket over her so she doesn't get cold. It's so chilly in here and they keep her in nothing but a diaper just in case anything goes wrong. With nurses watching over her and oxygen going constantly, she's safe with a blanket.

"Thank you," I murmur, leaning down to place a kiss on Scout's soft cheek.

"You're going to be an incredible mom, Samara."

I freeze, still bent over the bed. *Mom?*

"I'm not..." I clear my throat, standing up slowly. "I'm not a mom."

"You are now, honey," Carly says, giving me a gentle look. "I know she's your niece and you just lost your sister, but whether Scout calls you aunt or mom or something else, you're the only mom this little girl is ever going to know." She squeezes my arm. "You should know we all think you're going to be amazing with her."

"I...thank you," I whisper, not sure what else to say.

"I just thought you should know that we're all rooting for you," she says. "We see a lot of patients through here. I wish they all had caregivers like you." She presses a button on Scout's IV machine to restart one of the medications and then glances at me over her shoulder. "Dr. Grimes wants to see you in the conference room. Do you remember how to get there?"

"Yeah," I mumble.

"I'll watch Scout while you're meeting with him."

"Thanks..." I stand there for a minute, my feet rooted in place before I finally manage to make them move. When they do, I stumble out of the room, moving blindly through the PICU and then out into the main hospital. My mind swirls in a thousand different directions, but it moves too quickly for me to keep up with any of it.

By the time I reach the conference room, I feel...unsettled.

"Hey," Tate says, grinning at me when I step inside. He's sitting at the head of the massive table, one booted foot propped up on top. Unlike most of the doctors here, Tate doesn't dress like a surgeon. His black boots and jeans stand out beneath his white coat, but no one even bats a lash. I don't think anyone tells Tate what to do. He really is a man apart, playing by his own rules.

Everyone here likes him though. They respect him. When he says jump, they jump, no questions asked. He could be a jerk about it, and yet he's not. He's down-to-earth. Cocky, yes. Maybe even a little arrogant at times. But he's a genuinely good man. One of the best I've ever met. He's kind, patient, full of compassion and decency. I've never met anyone like him before. I doubt I ever will again.

Why does that scare me so damn much?

"Hey," I say, glancing around the empty room. "What's going on?"

"Paperwork." He holds up a folder. "I want to get it out of the way tonight so you don't have to sign a bunch of shit in the morning."

"Oh." I shuffle toward the table.

He cocks his head to the side, frowning. "What's wrong?"

"Nothing."

"Liar. What's wrong?"

"Nothing." I shake my head, forcing a smile. "I'm just tired."

I can tell he doesn't believe me, but he doesn't force the issue. He lets the subject drop for the moment, nudging a chair with his foot. "Sit down, angel," he says. "Let's get this out of the way so we can get you back to our girl."

"Our girl?"

He grins at me. "I plan on being her third favorite person behind you and Siobhan."

"Oh." I drop down into the chair, my stomach fluttering and churning. He's so good to her already. He calls constantly to check on her. I know he's checking on me too. The nurses have commented on it. I'm not sure what to tell them though, so I just shrug off their curiosity. "Um, what do I need to sign?"

"Consent forms," he says, flipping open the folder. "They say you understand there are risks and that things could go wrong. If they do go wrong, they say you understand that we'll do everything we can but there are no guarantees. These also give us permission to make decisions back there based on our judgement without having to delay by calling you to ask for input."

"Okay," I say, reaching for the pen.

He stops me, placing his hand over mine. "We have to talk before you sign, baby. I can't just let you sign until you know what could go wrong," he says quietly.

"I... No," I say, shaking my head. "I already know what's at risk, Tate. I know...I know she could die tomorrow. But I also know if I don't sign these and you don't operate, she *will* die. So whatever risks there are tomorrow, I accept them. I have to accept them."

"Death isn't the only risk, Samara," he says.

"I know, but it's the only one that's inevitable if you don't do this surgery." I take a deep breath, trying to calm my nerves. I've never told anyone my story before, but I want to tell him. "My whole life, it was just me and Siobhan. We grew up dirt poor with an alcoholic mom. We ended up in foster care more times than I can count. When our mom was sober enough to get us back from the system, we lived on the kindness of strangers and whatever abusive boyfriend she was dating at the time. She certainly wasn't sober enough to remember to feed us half the time."

"Jesus," Tate whispers.

"I know what it's like to have nothing because I came from nothing," I say. "All I had was Siobhan. Now, she's gone too. So it doesn't matter what the risks are, Tate. Not when the only person I ever had left her daughter in my care. She trusted me to save her baby, no matter what. I *won't* fail her now. I can't. Scout is the only thing I have left."

Tate watches me for a moment, his eyes bright. And then he curses softly. "Not anymore, angel," he says, gripping the back of my neck. "You have me."

I exhale a shaky breath. He's right. I know he is. And that scares the crap out of me. I feel like the world keeps shifting beneath my feet. As soon as I think I've caught my balance, it shifts again, sending me into another tailspin. I'm falling in love with this man, dangerously fast. Or maybe I'm already in love with him. The latter, I think. But I don't know how to process that right now, not when Scout needs me to be strong for her.

"I'm terrified I'm going to mess up," I admit. "Carly called me a mom a few minutes ago and it just...freaked me out. I don't know how to be a mom. I'm still learning how to be an aunt."

"Then be an aunt first," he says, lifting me out of my chair and into his lap. He wraps his arms around me, tucking my head against his chest. "No one said you had to figure it all out in one day. You'll fuck up and make mistakes. You aren't perfect. No parent is. But you love that little girl with your whole heart, and you want what's best for her."

"I do," I whisper.

"That's what it means to be a parent, Samara. I've seen you fight harder for her in two days than most people will fight for anything in their entire lives. It doesn't matter what you call yourself, you've already got that part down, baby."

"You think so?"

"I know so," he says, pressing his lips to the top of my head. "She's going to love you as fiercely as you love her."

"I'm terrified I'm going to lose her, Tate."

"Hey." He tips my head back, forcing me to look at him. "Do you trust me, Samara?"

"I..." I look into his dark emerald eyes. Do I trust him? "I think... I think I trust you more than I've ever trusted anyone before," I admit, swallowing hard. Isn't that what really scares me? I trust him when I've never trusted anyone, not like this.

"Then trust that I'm not going to let you lose her. Trust that I'm going to fight just as hard for her in that operating room tomorrow as you've been fighting all week. You're not alone in this anymore. I'm right here, Samara. I'm right here."

I press my lips to his, kissing him hard.

"You're hogging her," I complain, pouting at Tate.

"You told me I could hold her."

"I changed my mind. Give her back."

He chuckles, shaking his head. "No can do," he says, patting her gently on the back. "I think I'll keep her for a little while. She seems to like me."

I narrow my eyes on him, wondering if I'm allowed to have Daisy kick him out. Visiting hours ended a while ago. Since he's not technically here on business, surely that means he shouldn't be allowed in here, right? I'm not sure. I decide not to risk it. Just in case Daisy decides to make me leave too.

"Fine," I mutter instead, scowling. "But she still likes me more than you."

Tate chuckles again. "Angel, not a man alive would blame her for that," he drawls, shaking his head. "You're soft and sweet and perfect. I'm just a man with steady hands and a big c–"

"Don't you dare," I hiss, whipping my head around to make sure Daisy isn't in earshot.

"–erebellum." He cocks a brow. "What did you think I was going to say?"

I blush.

"In the hospital, Samara? Really?"

"You say dirty things wherever you want," I mutter defensively.

"I don't curse around the kids, Samara," he says, his voice soft. "My mom would throw a holy fit if she found out."

"You're scared of your mom?" I smile at him, my voice soft. Why is it so cute that this giant man is afraid of his mom?

"Uh, yeah. Are you kidding me? My dad would kick my A-S-S if I wasn't afraid of my mom," he says, looking at me like I'm crazy. "No one stresses her out without answering to him, especially me and my twin."

My mouth pops open. "You have a twin?"

"I do. His name is Xavier. He and Sariah, my older sister, live in Los Angeles near our parents."

"Wow," I whisper. "Are they doctors too?"

"They work in the fashion industry. My dad is a photographer. My mom owns a modeling agency. Xavier and Sariah help her run it."

"I didn't know that."

He smiles at me. "You'll love them."

"You...want me to meet them?" My stomach flips.

"They'll be out here in September. They come every year."

"Oh," I whisper, not sure what to say. But I think...I think I'm looking forward to it. I want to know where Tate came from. I want to meet the people who raised and shaped him. It doesn't take a genius to know they have to be pretty amazing. "I'd like that."

"Yeah?"

His cocky grin has me rolling my eyes.

"Give me back my niece before I change my mind," I demand, ready to hold her again. It's purely selfish, but I know Tate doesn't mind. He's only holding onto her to annoy me. He seems to like doing that. I'll never admit it, but I kind of like it too. It's hard to stress and worry and panic when I'm with him. He refuses to let me.

It's as if he just instinctively knows how to calm me down. He doesn't even have to try. As soon as I start feeling anxious, he reaches for me or says something ridiculous. Immediately, my nerves settle and a sense of calm washes over me. I have no idea how I'm going to make it through tomorrow without him at my side, but I'll find a way. Even if I crack apart at the seams.

Tate's phone vibrates in his pocket.

He gently shifts Scout around and then reaches for it.

"You're in luck," he says, giving it a cursory glance. "I have something to take care of, so I'll let you hold her while I do it."

"Let me hold her?" I splutter. "She's my niece."

He smirks at me, shaking his head. He doesn't say anything as he rises to his feet with Scout tucked carefully in his arms. Because she's sedated, she doesn't even twitch. The nurses assure me that she knows we're here with her and that she can hear us, but she doesn't really respond to much. I can't wait until her little eyes open. I hope they're hazel like Siobhan's.

Tate places her carefully in my arms and then runs his hand over the top of her head, smoothing her wild hair. "I'm not sure what you aren't getting, angel," he says, tipping my head back until our gazes tangle. "She might be your niece, but you're both *mine.*" He leans down, pressing his lips to mine in a hard kiss. "Cuddle our girl. I'll be right back."

When he straightens, I see Daisy standing in the doorway, watching us. My stomach flutters with nerves at being caught, but she just smiles at us.

"Take care of my girls for me," he orders her, winking on his way out the door.

"Yes, sir," she says, laughing quietly.

I bury my face in Scout's hair, trying to hide my flaming cheeks. I'm not sure what the rules are about doctors dating the family members of patients, but I'm sure they probably have a few of them. I'm also guessing Tate doesn't give a crap about them. No one tells him what to do. It's one of the things I love about him.

Crap, I love him. So damn much.

Should I tell him? I should, shouldn't I? He deserves to know that, regardless of what happens tomorrow, I love him. Not because of what happens in the operating room tomorrow but because of who he is. Because it's impossible *not* to love him. I know because I tried so hard not to fall for him. But I'm tired of being afraid.

This crazy, amazing man chose me, and I'm choosing him back. If he's all in, then I am too. No matter what happens tomorrow, I want him to know that my heart belongs to him.

"His girls, huh?" Daisy shoots me a grin, one brow arched in question.

"Um..." I dart a worried glance around. "Can he get in any trouble for this?"

"Honestly?" Daisy shrugs. "I'm sure there are those who would say it's unethical, but everyone here loves Dr. Grimes. If you two are happy, we're happy for you. You won't hear any complaints from us. Happiness can be fleeting in a place like this. We take it where it comes."

"Thanks," I whisper, relaxing as that fear eases. I know eventually being with him will mean finding a new doctor for Scout. He can't be ours and be her surgeon forever. But for tomorrow, at least, there's no one else I trust more than I do him.

I relax into the seat, cuddling Scout close as Daisy bustles around, changing out her sheets. My eyes drift closed. I focus on Scout's breathing, on the steady rise and fall off her little chest against mine.

Watch over her tomorrow, Siobhan, I pray. *Keep her safe one more time.*

"Hey," Tate says a few minutes later.

My eyes flutter open.

"Oh my gosh," I gasp, staring in shock. Troian and Gage fill the doorway behind Tate. Daisy's seated at her desk outside the door. Gage has his arm around his curvy wife. They're both smiling at me. "What are you guys doing here?"

"Tate thought you could use some company to-morrow," Troian says, squeezing past him into the room. She hurries to my side, leaning down to hug me with one arm. "She's beautiful, Samara."

"I'm so glad you're here," I say, my voice thick with emotion.

"Of course we're here," she whispers back. "You're my best friend. Where else would I be?"

"So this is Miss Scout," Gage says when Troian steps back. He leans down to kiss me on the cheek. "How are you holding up, sweetheart? Is this jackal being good to you?"

"So good," I whisper, meeting Tate's warm gaze over his head. He grins at me, his expression soft.

"Good," Gage says, winking at me. "Troian would be pissed if she had to bail me out of jail for punching him in the face tonight."

"I already told you I wouldn't bail you out," Troian says, scrunching up her face at him. "You'll just have to stay there while Scout and I hang out tonight."

"You and Scout?" I blink at her.

She just smiles a mysterious smile.

"She and Gage are going to stay with Scout tonight, angel," Tate says, stepping deeper into the room. His gaze tangles with mine. "I know you won't sleep without someone here."

"Oh." My heart flutters wildly again. "I was going to stay."

"No can do," Troian says, her voice firm. "You're going back to Tate's tonight. You're sleeping in a real bed. You can stay with her tomorrow after her surgery. Tonight, Gage and I will watch over her for you."

"I...thank you," I whisper, a lump rising in my throat. I was wrong earlier. Scout isn't all I have left. Not even close. Right now, I'm pretty sure I have almost everything.

CHAPTER SEVEN

Tate

"You're awful quiet," I say, watching Samara as she wanders aimlessly around the penthouse. She picks up a vase and then sets it down before moving to the bookcase. Her fingers trail along the spines of a row of books. Her mind is a million miles away.

It has been since we left the hospital an hour ago. She's anxious about tomorrow. I haven't told her yet that my brothers are coming. I'm not sure it'll help ease her mind any. Springing it on her is probably a dick move, but I'd rather pull a dick move than give her one more thing to fret over tonight.

She needs people in her corner tomorrow. If anything goes wrong, I want her surrounded by a wall of support until I can get to her. Between Troian, Gage, and my brothers, she'll be in good hands...and I need them there so I can do what I need to do. It's the only way I'll be able to focus on Scout and doing what I need to do to keep my promise.

There's a reason why surgeons don't operate on family. This is it. If there were anyone else capable of performing this surgery tomorrow, I'd step back and let them take over. But everyone else is hesitant to even try because Scout is so fragile. At this juncture, I'm her best hope...her only hope. So I'm performing the surgery in the morning. Once she's through it, we'll find her another doctor to take over, someone who knows what the fuck they're doing. But for now, that's me.

"Angel." I pace across the room toward Samara, linking our fingers together. "What are you thinking about?"

"You," she says, surprising me.

"Me?" I bring her fingers to my lips, kissing the pad of each one.

"You got Gage and Troian special approval to stay with Scout tonight," she says, staring at me with wide eyes. "You brought them here for me."

"I didn't want you to be alone tomorrow." I nip the pad of her thumb.

"You did it because you love me," she says, her voice strong, confident.

My lips tip up into a grin. "You're just figuring that out, huh?"

"No." She shakes her head. "I knew. I think I just found the courage to admit it to myself though." Her gaze flits across my face, her golden eyes filled with awe. "You love me."

"Yeah, I do," I whisper, tugging her closer to my body. "So if that freaks you out, I'm going to need you to get over it. Because it's not going to change anytime soon. My heart beats for you now. Whether you want me or not, I'm yours. I'll chase you to the ends of the earth if that's what it takes to make you see that you belong with me."

"What if..." She trails off, licking her lips. "What if...?"

"What if what?"

"What if I already see it?" Her breath trembles against my lips. "What if I already know I'm yours, Tate?" She pulls her hand from mine, lacing both of hers together around my neck. "What if I already love you back?"

"Fuck," I growl, gripping her hips in my hands. "Don't say it if you don't mean it, Samara."

She lifts up on her toes, her lips skimming across my jaw toward my ear. "I love you, Tate Grimes," she whispers in my ear. "I love you. I love you. I love—"

I cut her off, covering her mouth with mine. She topples into my chest with a soft cry, allowing me to lick my way into her mouth. I steal her breath, pulling her air into my lungs, swallowing her sounds down my throat. My hands flex around her hips as I fight for control. Every part of me wants to sweep her up into my arms, carry her into the bedroom, and make her mine. But it's a purely selfish desire...and I can't be selfish with her.

"Come on," I murmur, reluctantly breaking the kiss before I lose what little willpower I have. With her, it's so fucking easy to get carried away. As soon as I get my hands on her, the rest of the world falls away, narrowing to her and the feel of her beautiful body against mine. I forget everything else. But I can't do that tonight. She needs me to take care of her tonight, to be strong for her and Scout.

I lift her into my arms, carrying her through the penthouse into the bedroom. I stop long enough to hit the button to close the blinds over the windows, and then continue on into the bathroom. She settles against the vanity with a soft murmur.

"Easy," I say, brushing my lips across her temple.

I leave her long enough to start the shower. Hot water pours from the shower heads, steam billowing through the room.

"Jesus," I mutter, my heart rolling when I turn back to her. She looks like a water nymph perched on the vanity, wisps of steam dancing around her flushed face.

"What are you doing?" She watches me through slit lids, a soft, adoring smile on her face as I undress. Her golden eyes kiss my skin like a brand everywhere they touch. I feel them on me, searing me with her possession, with her light.

"Loving you," I say, prowling across the heated floor toward her. My mouth meets hers. We kiss once. Twice. A third time. I'm addicted to her mouth. As soon as I stop kissing it, I want to start all over again. No one warned me about this part of falling in love, the constant craving for contact. It's enthralling, consuming. I love every fucking thing about it.

Somehow, I manage to strip her between kisses. I run my hands down her body, touching her everywhere. I've held the smallest, most fragile hearts in my hands, and felt awe that something so small could be so powerful. I've been humbled and overjoyed, fought for the impossible and somehow prevailed. But nothing compares to the softness of her skin against my fingertips. Nothing compares to knowing this incredible woman trusts me with her heart.

I boost her into my arms, her legs around my waist. Our mouths meet again, tongues dancing together as I carry her into the shower. My dick is hard enough to hurt, but this isn't about him. It's about her.

The sound of pure bliss that tumbles from her lips when the hot water envelopes us will haunt every dream I have for the next five decades. She turns to putty in my arms.

I slide her down my body to her feet, anchoring her to me with one arm. "Relax," I whisper against her temple. "Let me take care of you tonight."

She hums a wordless agreement, practically purring in my arms. Fuck. I can't wait to spoil her like this every day. She's been on her own for so damn long, far longer than she should have been. She was just a kid, worrying about when she was going to eat or where she would sleep, seeing horrors no child should ever see.

No more, I vow, reaching for the shampoo. *Never again.* For the rest of her life, she won't have to worry about shit like that. She'll know every day that she and Scout are wanted, needed, and loved. She will never be alone, ever again.

"I love you," I say, digging my fingers into her scalp to massage the shampoo in. "You and Scout are going to be my whole world, angel."

"Yeah?" She turns to face me, tipping her head back into the shower spray. Shampoo cascades down her curvy body, covering her with soap. Her satisfied, womanly smile has my balls throbbing for release. She reaches between us, running her knuckles over my dick. "Show me what it means to be yours, Tate."

"Samara, angel," I groan. "You don't owe me this. I can wait."

"I can't," she whispers, wrapping one perfect hand around my shaft. "We both know you won't be able to drag me away from the hospital after tomorrow, Tate. Not until Scout's okay. I don't want to wait weeks to be yours when I know part of me will die a little every day without you. I need you to make me whole now so I can be strong for Scout later."

"You're already the strongest woman I know," I groan, my willpower crumbling. If she wants this, who the hell am I to tell her no? She can have anything. Anything. I'd crawl through hell on my knees to give it to her. "Are you sure?"

"I've never been more sure of anything," she says.

"Fuck." I tip my head forward, letting my resolve fall to ruins. It lands at our feet and then swirls down the drain, washed away like papier-mâché. I take her mouth in a deep kiss, claiming her, possessing her, ruining her too.

She moans, pressing her tits up against my chest. I reach blindly for the soap, using it to slick up my hands. We kiss again and again as I wash her, touching her everywhere. I pay extra attention to her hard little nipples, playing with them until she's whimpering my name.

She's soaked when I slip my hand between her legs to clean her there. I play with her, exploring every fold, learning every one of her secrets. The soap is gone long before I push her up against the wall and throw her legs over my shoulders.

She screams in shock, clutching handfuls of my hair like she's afraid I'll let her fall. That will never happen.

I make a mess of the pussy I just cleaned, using my lips and tongue to drive her wild. Her cries echo around the bathroom, growing louder and then louder still. By the time I work the tip of my tongue into her tasty little asshole, she cracks with a shrill scream of ecstasy, coating my face with her cream.

She's still coming when I stand upright, yanking her into my arms. I barely stop long enough to turn off the water before stepping out of the shower and reaching for a towel. I dry her carefully, running the fluffy towel all over her still trembling body.

"Tate," she moans.

"I know, angel."

"You..."

"I know."

"That wasn't my vagina," she whisper-hisses.

"I'm well aware, Samara."

She huffs at me.

"Don't pretend you didn't scream the roof down around us when I had my tongue in your tasty little asshole, Samara," I growl, tossing the towel toward the hamper. "We both know you loved every second of it."

She's quiet for a second. "Well, yeah," she finally mumbles, too damn cute for words. "But I don't think you're supposed to say that."

I laugh quietly, dropping her gently on the bed. "On your back, baby. Legs spread. I want to see what's mine before I take that sweet cherry."

"Bossy."

"I already told you, I'm *the* boss. Now, be a good girl and do what you're told."

"Yes, *Doctor* Grimes."

I narrow my eyes and growl, making her laugh. She does what she's told though, scooting up the bed and then flopping down on her back. She shyly parts her legs until her glistening pussy peeps from between her thighs. Her clit is hard and swollen.

"Damn," I breathe, fisting my cock. Once Scout is better, I'm taking her to Angel's island paradise. Gloria can babysit for a week while I keep this woman naked and on my cock. If I'm lucky, I'll plant my kid in her, give her another baby to love just like she loves Scout. "I don't know where to start with you."

"Right here," she says, lifting her arms in silent entreaty.

I stalk toward the bed, hers to command. I may pretend to make the rules, but we both know she has me by the balls here. I'm her willing subject, her helpless acolyte. I prowl over her gorgeous little body, her lips curving into a smile.

"Beautiful," I whisper, kissing my way up her legs. My breathing picks up when she moans my name and spreads her legs further in invitation. I kiss and nibble on her thighs, breathing in her sweet scent. When I die, if it's not buried face first in her cunt, it'll be a waste.

"I need to taste you again, angel," I say, tossing her legs over my shoulders. Before she can respond, I lick from her ass to her clit. As soon as her taste hits my system, I growl. Jesus. I'm addicted to this pussy. I swear, it gets sweeter every time I eat it. Wetter too.

I take my time with her this time, eating her like I have all night. Every drop she spills, I lick up, savoring it. My tongue runs in circles around her clit before teasing along the hood of it. I pull each juicy lip into my mouth and suck on it before thrusting my tongue into her opening. She whines, grinding her pussy against my face.

Fuck, I need her to come.

I work two fingers inside her, fighting like hell the entire time. She's virgin tight, her body making me work for it. By the time I finally get them in, I'm grinding my hips into the mattress, trying not to lose my damn mind. I curl my fingers up to rub her g-spot, sucking her clit into my mouth at the same time. As soon as I do, she shouts my name, coming all over my face.

I lick up every drop, working her through it. My dick leaks cum all over the comforter, leaving a sticky mess. I don't fucking care. This right here...this is as close to heaven as I've ever been. I don't stop what I'm doing to her until she's writhing beneath me again, well on her way to another orgasm. Once her pussy starts fluttering again, I back off, prowling up her body.

"You stopped," she pouts, her golden eyes dilated, and her cheeks flushed.

"I need in you," I murmur, kissing the pout from her lips. "Are you ready for me?"

"Yes. No." She squeezes her eyes closed and swallows hard. "Yes."

"I'll fit," I remind her, touching my forehead to hers as I pull her leg up over my hip. And then I freeze. "Fuck. I don't have a condom."

"Oh no," she whispers. "Are you...? Have you been tested?"

Have I been tested?

"I haven't been with anyone else, angel," I say, a little surprised she doesn't already know. I thought she knew what I meant when I told her that no one else touches me.

She blinks wide, startled eyes at me. "You're a virgin?"

"You'll be my first and only," I murmur.

"Tate," she whispers, her voice soft.

"I was waiting for you." I nudge my nose with hers. "I feel like I've been waiting for you my entire life, Sleeping Beauty."

"Me too," she says, reaching up to touch my cheek. "Um, I'm on birth control."

A growl starts in my chest.

"It's not like that." She rolls her eyes. "Calm down, bossy. My periods are weird. I take it to help regulate them. That's all. I haven't even been on a date since I was in high school."

"Angel, stop talking before you piss me off," I growl, pressing my lips to hers. "Other men don't exist to you. I don't care if it was in elementary school. It never happened."

"Tate? Stop being crazy and make love to me," she demands, smiling at me.

"Kiss me," I order, not sure how to make this more comfortable for her. It's going to hurt no matter what I do. She's tiny and I'm...not. I send up a quick prayer that I manage to last long enough to make it good for her. As badly as I want her right now, it's entirely possible this ends before it even begins.

She chases my lips with hers, seaming our mouths together. We kiss for several long moments, sinking into one another slowly. I run my hands up and down her sides, trying to relax her as much as possible. My dick slides through her soaked folds, bumping against her clit with every pass. I'm dying the sweetest death with every second that passes, but I don't rush it. I take my time. I make her take hers. Only when she's pliant beneath me, moans leaving her lips in little puffs of sound, do I line up at her entrance.

"Ah, fuck," I groan, pushing my way into her wet heat. Her pussy surrounds the head of my cock, burning hot. She's so damn soft and warm. So tight. I push forward slowly, my eyes locked on her face, watching for any signs of discomfort. At first, all I see is awe swirling through those golden depths.

The head of my cock slips in.

I writhe, fighting not to come. Christ, she feels good. Too good, maybe.

I push forward again, meeting resistance.

Awe turns to hesitation, anxiety flitting through her expression.

"Kiss me, angel," I demand.

"Tate."

"Kiss me, Samara."

She offers her mouth up like an obedient little sacrifice.

"I love you," I whisper, covering her mouth with mine.

I push forward. Her hymen resists for a split second before tearing around my cock. She cries out in shock, going completely rigid beneath me. I sink into her to the hilt. My stomach churns with regret, my balls with relief.

"I'm sorry," I breathe, kissing her lips again and then again. "I'm sorry."

She whimpers into my mouth, the pained sound breaking my heart.

"Never again," I vow, kissing all over her face. "It'll never feel like that again, angel."

"Good because that hurt," she says, sniffling. "I told you that you wouldn't fit."

"Angel, baby." I groan, trying not to laugh because I'm pretty sure that will just piss her off. "I'm inside that juicy cunt right now, buried all the way to the hilt."

Her pussy spasms around me.

Interesting.

"You're taking all of me, Samara," I say, placing my mouth near her ear. "And as soon as you're ready, I'm going to ride that pretty pussy until you're coming all over my cock."

Her pussy spasms again.

Oh, angel. I know your number now. She likes the dirty talk.

"I think I'm ready now," she whispers.

"Yeah?" I nip at her ear and then wrap my tongue around the lobe to ease the sting of my bite. "Maybe I should keep saying filthy shit to you just to make sure. I could tell you how good you taste when you're coming all over my tongue. Or how much you're going to like it when you're on your hands and knees next time with that ass in the air and I'm drilling you from behind." I nuzzle my face into her neck, kissing and nipping at her skin. "Or maybe I should tell you how fucking hard I got when you were gagging on my cock last night."

Her pussy clamps down on me hard this time.

"Tate," she moans, her hands drifting down my back.

"Yeah," I chuckle. "You're ready."

"Then f-fuck me already!" she cries.

"Nu-uh," I whisper, shaking my head against hers. "When I'm in you, I'm making love to you, Samara. It doesn't matter how filthy my mouth is or what kinky shit I do to you, I will never take you with anything less than complete reverence." I brush my mouth against hers, hitching her leg higher up my hip. "When I'm in you, I plan to worship you. Every single time."

"Oh my gosh," she whispers.

I rock my hips back and then push forward, taking her slowly. She needs to know this isn't fucking. It doesn't matter how dirty it gets, there's nothing casual about this for either one of us. This woman is my soul, the one I've been waiting for my entire life. I fully intend to spend the rest of it loving her the way she deserves. She doesn't know what it's like to be loved unconditionally, to have a place in this world and people to call her own. She will with me.

"Oh," she gasps, grasping onto my shoulders. "Oh my god."

"That's right," I croon, kissing a trail down her throat. "In this bed, I'm your god. You ride my cock to heaven." I pull her nipple into my mouth, raking it through my teeth. "It's yours anyway. Every part of me is yours."

"Tate," she cries, writhing beneath me.

I make love to her slowly, pumping my hips like we have all night. I feel her walls dragging against my cock with every thrust, feel the way they clench and flutter and grip me tight. She's heaven around me, the most incredible thing I've ever experienced. And still, I want to go deeper, until I'm imprinted inside her, a permanent piece of her.

I flip her to her stomach, coming down over her. My thighs spread hers wide, my body caging hers in on the bed. She melts into the mattress, her wet hair tangled in my fist. I kiss all over her neck and shoulders, grinding my hips against her round ass. I'm deeper this way, the head of my cock nudging against her cervix with every thrust.

My name leaves her lips in an endless chant as she undulates beneath me, arching and bowing, giving herself over to me and the sheer pleasure of it. Her sweet cries of ecstasy spur me on. I fuck her harder, my lips never leaving her skin as my balls tap against her ass in steady smacks.

"I love you, Samara," I whisper. "My Sleeping Beauty. My warrior angel."

"Tate," she cries. "I...I..."

Whatever she was going to say gets lost as her body bows...and breaks. Her pussy clamps down on my cock in a stranglehold, my name echoing from the rafters as she shatters apart beneath me.

I roar her name, my own orgasm ripped from me by the force of hers. I don't stand a chance of holding it off. Cum shoots up my shaft, my balls emptying into her in pulses that leave me trembling above her.

For one perfect moment, we find eternity together.

It's better than I ever imagined it could be.

When it's over, I fall beside her, dragging her into my arms.

"I'm keeping you," I whisper, holding her close to my heart. "You and Scout are mine to love now, mine to protect."

"Okay," she breathes, already sinking into sleep. "Whatever you say, bossy."

Chapter Eight

Samara

"Angel," Tate says, squatting in front of me.

I glance up from Scout, my heart skipping two beats at the serious look in his eyes.

"It's time to go," he says, his voice soft.

For a split second, my grip on Scout tightens as fear and anxiety short circuit my mind. I have to physically force myself to relax my grip on her and nod, letting him know I understand. I press my face to Scout's little head and take a deep breath, fighting not to cry.

"Tate's going to take good care of you now, baby girl," I whisper. "Don't be afraid." I press my lips to her head and linger for a long moment, sending up a silent prayer. When I was a kid, I used to pray for my mom to stop drinking. It never worked, so I figured either God didn't answer prayers from girls like me, or he just didn't care.

I'm not even sure if there is a God at this point, but I started praying again when I found out about Scout. If someone is up there, I think they're listening now. I feel it in my soul. Whether it's God or Siobhan or something else, I don't know. But I pray anyway. Harder than I ever have before.

My hands shake when I hand her over to Jules, Tate's surgery nurse.

"We'll take good care of her," Jules promises, laying her gently in the small bed they'll wheel her into the OR room in. She gives me a confident smile. "I'll call you with updates as often as possible."

"Thank you." My voice trembles.

"Give us a minute," Tate says, glancing at Jules and the anesthesiologist over his shoulder.

"We'll wait in the hall with Scout," Jules says.

I watch with my heart in my throat as they wheel her out of the room.

Tate waits until they're gone and then rises to his feet, pulling me up to mine. His strong arms surround me, cradling me against his chest. "I have a private waiting room set up for you, angel," he murmurs. "One of the nurses will escort you out to it."

"Thank you."

"Gage and Troian are waiting for you out there."

"Okay."

He hesitates.

"So are my brothers from the MC."

I pull back to look at him.

"Don't be afraid," he says, his expression somber. "They wanted to be here to support you."

"I... Really?" I ask, shellshocked that they're here.

He nods, bumping his forehead against mine. "You're family now, angel. What happens to one of us happens to all of us. I'd like you to meet them. If you'd rather them wait in the main waiting room after that, they're willing to do that. They'll give you as much space as you need, but they wanted to be here anyway."

Guilt whispers through me, humbling me. I was so quick to judge them. Now that I know Tate and the kind of man he is, I *know* how unfair I was to assume every MC was like the one that killed Siobhan. If Tate trusts his brothers, I trust his brothers. How can I not? There isn't a cruel bone in Tate's body, and he would never associate himself with men capable of doing such horrible things.

"They don't have to do that," I say, shaking my head. "I want to meet them."

"Are you sure?" he asks. "I don't want to push, angel. Not today."

"I want to meet them," I say again, meaning it.

"My fierce little angel," he whispers, pressing his lips to my forehead. "As soon as surgery is finished, I'll be out to find you."

"I know." I squeeze him tight. "D-do everything you can."

"Everything," he vows, his promise reflecting in his eyes. "I love you."

"I love you too."

He releases me and ducks out of the room. I squeeze my eyes closed, not nearly brave enough to watch my whole heart disappear down the hall.

Please, I pray. *Please.*

A few seconds later, Rhonda, one of the surgery nurses, steps into the pre-op holding room. "You ready, sweetheart?" she asks, giving me a kind smile. "Dr. Grimes asked me to show you out to the family waiting room where he's got your crew corralled."

I glance around the small, windowless room and then nod helplessly. Even though I tell myself I'm not going to look, I find myself peeking down every hallway, looking for Tate and Scout. By the time Rhonda swipes her badge in front of the double doors that bar entry into the surgery suite from the waiting rooms, I haven't seen them.

"You're in here," she says, leading me to the hallway on the right. She pauses outside of a heavy oak door. The low murmur of hushed conversation spills out from within. "There's a coffee station inside and a small snack bar. Lucinda at the front desk knows you're in here. When Jules calls with updates, she'll send them through to the phone back here."

"Thank you," I whisper.

She squeezes my elbow. "Good luck, sweetheart. We're all rooting for Scout."

I swallow hard but don't respond. If I do, I think I might cry. I'd rather not do that right now. Not with Tate's brothers waiting on the other side of the door. Not with Scout in surgery. I'll cry later, once I know she's okay.

Taking a deep breath, I push the door open.

The waiting room is spacious...or it would be if it weren't packed with bodies. Tate's brothers are as big as he is, some even bigger. Troian looks like a little kid next to them. She's not the only woman in the room. A middle-aged woman with gray hair and a motherly smile stands beside the coffee station, passing out cups. A curvy blonde is cuddled up with a dark-haired hunk, listening intently to a giant of a man with a pirate's smile and a wicked gleam in his eyes.

Two men in suits are deep in conversation with a middle-aged man on the far side of the room. He keeps one watchful eye on the woman standing by the coffee pot. A hunk in a t-shirt and glasses, another man in a suit, and one in worn Wranglers and a cowboy hat stand next to her, talking quietly to Gage. Another man stands off to the side, his head bent over his phone. A veritable giant leans against the wall next to him, one booted heel planted against the wall.

Everyone falls silent when they see me. Troian gives me an encouraging smile.

"Hi," I squeak, wringing my hands together.

The hunk with the blonde steps forward to meet me, his dark eyes running over me. "Hi, sweetheart," he says, his voice soft. His expression too. "I'm Jason Montoya, but you can call me Cash. You're Tate's girl?"

"I...Yeah," I whisper, licking my lips. "I'm Samara."

"Hi, Samara," he says, giving me a little smile. "You holding up okay?"

I nod, not sure that's true. I feel like I could crack apart at any minute.

I think Jason...Cash...knows it. His expression softens further. He takes another step toward me, moving slowly, as if he's afraid to startle me.

"If you'd rather be alone today, we can wait in the main waiting room," he says, still speaking quietly. "But we wanted to let you know that we're here if you need anything. You and your niece are important to Hands." He grimaces. "Tate, I mean. That makes you family to every man in this room. We aren't like most MCs, but we always protect our family, Samara. Understand?"

"I understand."

He examines my face for a moment, and then shakes his head, smiling. "You don't, not yet. But you will, sweetheart."

"Do I get to hug her now?" The giant booms.

"Fuck no," Cash snaps, sending a ripple of laughter through the room. Even Troian and Gage laugh.

"Ah, come on," the giant complains. "I've been waiting years to watch Hands turn into a territorial bastard. Don't ruin my fun now."

"I'm not helping him hide your big ass body, Giant," one of the other brothers murmurs. "I've got enough shit to deal with already."

"He couldn't take me," Giant grins, flashing two dimples.

"Trust me," one of the brothers in a suit says, his blue eyes locked on me. There's something in his gaze that's almost...sad. "He could take you."

"Do you want me to kick them out, Samara?" Cash asks.

"I...no," I say, quickly shaking my head.

He can't hide his surprise, even though he masks it quickly.

"Please stay," I whisper, a little afraid he's going to make them leave anyway. I don't want that. Tate asked me to get to know them, and I want to do that. After everything he's done for me, I owe it to him to give these men a chance. I owe it to them too. I think I owe it to myself and Scout too.

Cash hesitates for a brief moment and then nods.

"Then let me introduce you," he says, motioning me forward. "Come here, kitten."

The blonde steps forward to meet us.

"Samara, this is my wife, Hadley."

"Hi," Hadley says, giving me a sweet smile. Her blue eyes swim with empathy, her expression warm and open. She seems nice. Not fake nice, but genuinely nice. I immediately like her. "It's really nice to meet you, Samara."

"You too," I whisper. "Um, thank you for coming today."

"Anytime," she says, and I know it's not just a platitude. She means it.

Cash starts introducing the brothers at the back of the room, pointing to the man in the suit who said Tate could take Giant. "That's Jude Despora," Cash says. "We call him Fifth."

"Nice to meet you, Samara," Jude says, giving me a smile.

"Hi," I whisper.

"Next is Andreas Romano, Playboy."

Andreas flashes me a smile, not saying anything. He looks a lot like Cash, only with an olive skin tone and a hardness in his eyes that Cash lacks. All the brothers seem like they come from money, but Andreas more than most.

"I'm Rulie," the middle-aged guy beside Andreas says, lifting his hand in a two-finger salute. "The gorgeous woman by the coffee pot is my old lady, Gloria."

"It's nice to meet you both," I whisper, smiling. I like him instantly.

"I'm Rafe," the guy beside Gloria says, lifting his hand in a wave. "You can call me Lynch. Like Andreas and Jude, he's dressed in a suit.

"Hi, Rafe."

"Landon," the hunk in the cowboy hat drawls, winking at me. "Everyone calls me Cowboy."

"Beside him is Finn," Cash says, introducing the guy in a t-shirt and glasses. "We call him Hacker."

"Hey, Samara," Finn says, his lips curving into a smile.

"I'm Cormac," Giant says, flashing me that pirate's smile. I already know he's trouble with a capital T. But I don't think he's a bad guy. Just a handful. His nickname certainly fits him.

"And this," Cash says, turning to the last man in the room, "is His Royal Highness, Damien De Angelis. We call him Angel."

"More like His Royal Pain in the Ass," Rafe mutters, earning grins from his brothers.

"His Royal Highness?"

"Angel is the Crown Prince of Belldonnia," Cash says, grinning.

"Oh, wow," I say, fidgeting. "Um, I've never met royalty before. Am I supposed to bow or curtsey or something?"

"Fuck no," Damien growls, his deep voice slightly accented. "I come here to get away from all of that. These assholes just like to give me shit about it." He scowls at Cash before turning back to me. "It's nice to meet you, Samara. Though I wish it were under better circumstances."

"Me too." I glance around the room at everyone, powerful emotion swelling in my chest. For the first time in a long time, maybe for the first time ever, I don't feel alone. Because of Tate, Scout is surrounded by love and so I am.

Tears of gratitude well in my eyes, spilling over before I can stop them.

"Thank you," I say as their faces blur. "All of you."

Half an hour later, the waiting begins in earnest. Jules calls to let me know that they're getting started. My hands shake when I hang up the phone. They tremble so hard it takes two tries before I'm able to replace the receiver in the cradle.

Thirteen sets of eyes focus on me when I turn to face the room.

"They just got started," I say, my voice shaking as hard as my hands.

A murmur of unease ripples through the room as everyone tenses at once. I think I let every single one of these men into my heart right then and there. The fact that they care enough to worry about a baby they've never met speaks volumes about the kind of men they are. The fact that they're here at all does too. I'm sure they have a million things they'd rather do today than wait around a hospital, but they're here anyway.

Troian hops up from her seat beside Gage and hurries toward me.

She leads me toward a chair in the corner, gently urging me to sit.

I plop down, thrusting my hands into the pockets of Tate's oversized hoodie. I'm not sure if it's really freezing cold in here or if it's just me, but I feel like a block of ice sits on my chest. I close my eyes, imagining his arms around me instead of his hoodie. His heart beating beneath my ear, his hands running through my hair. Some ridiculous statement tumbling from his lips. He's probably a certified genius, but he says stupid stuff all the time, just to make me smile.

Even though he's in the operating room with Scout, I lean on him and his strength, letting him get me through this.

"Hi." Cash's wife, Hadley, slips into the seat beside me.

"Hey," I whisper, giving her the approximation of a smile. My leg bounces with nervous energy. It feels like it's been centuries since Jules called with the last update. I know it hasn't been that long, but time passes in dribbles, even with Tate's brothers here.

The sun rose hours ago, and then morning gave way to noon, which is slowly trickling by. The hands on the clock inch closer and closer to one. Tate's brothers haven't moved an inch. The waiting room is overrun with handsome men sprawled across uncomfortable chairs. Every single one of them looks like they're prepared to sit here as long as it takes. Trying not to cry in front of them is taking all of my concentration.

A giant crack opened up in my heart this morning. One side of it is crippled with worry. The other side though...seeing these men here now silently waiting for news about my niece...that side is stitching itself back together little by little.

Hadley is beautiful. Curvy, like me, with aqua eyes and freckles across the bridge of her nose. Her long blonde hair is up in a ponytail, keeping it out of her way. Like me, she's dressed in leggings and a hoodie. "Are you holding up okay?"

"Yes." I exhale a breath. "No."

She slips her hand into mine and squeezes. "It's terrifying, isn't it? Not knowing, I mean?"

"Yeah, it is," I say.

"I was in an accident a few weeks ago," she says, her voice soft so it doesn't carry. She lays her free hand on her stomach. "I'm pregnant with twins. We were afraid I was going to lose the babies. I still worry about it, but the twins are doing great so far." Her lips curve into a tiny smile. "Having Hands...um, Tate around helps. He's an amazing doctor. Your niece is in the best care possible with him."

"I know," I say, grateful to her for saying it because she's right. There isn't a single person in this world I trust more with Scout than I trust Tate. I just wish Jules would hurry and call with another update. It's been at least an hour and half, maybe longer.

"Cash told me what happened to your sister," Hadley says. "I'm so sorry, Samara."

"Thank you," I whisper.

"When Scout is better, if you'd like, we'd like to do something to honor her...I mean, if that's okay with you," she hurries to add. "What she did was really incredible, you know? I know you didn't really get a chance to celebrate her life the way you deserve to celebrate her. We want to help you do that. If it's okay?" She chews on her bottom lip like she's worried she may have overstepped and I'm going to freak out.

"I'd like that," I whisper around the lump in my throat as emotion courses through me. Siobhan's funeral was a sad, rushed affair. It was me, Troian, a preacher, and the detective assigned to her case. There was no time for the celebration she deserved, but I planned to do something more fitting after Scout was okay. If Hadley and Tate's brothers want to help, I'm not going to tell them no. It's a touching gesture. Aside from Tate, they're the first people I've met who haven't immediately assumed the worst about her.

That realization makes me squirm. For a week and a half, I've been so upset whenever doctors looked down their noses at me, silently judging Siobhan without knowing her story. They assumed the worst about her without even knowing what she went through, without knowing *her*. But I did the exact same thing to Tate and his brothers.

"I'm such a hypocrite," I say, feeling about two inches tall.

Hadley looks at me in question.

"I was...a jerk about MCs," I admit, staring at my hands. "I judged them so harshly after what happened to Siobhan. But you guys have been so good to me and Scout. Tate has been so good to us."

"You aren't a hypocrite," Hadley says, squeezing my hand again. "You lost your sister, Samara. You're allowed to be angry and frightened and confused. Anyone would be. Despite everything, you still gave Tate a chance. You still gave us a chance. That takes courage."

"I don't feel very brave," I mutter. Right now, I feel the exact opposite of brave.

"I know a certain surgeon who would beg to differ," she says, grinning at me.

Before I can respond, the door to the waiting room opens.

My breath stalls in my throat.

Tate steps into the room, dressed in scrubs, a green cap on his head, matching green booties on his feet. His emerald eyes immediately come to me, his expression somber. I can't tell if it's good news or bad news.

I jump to my feet. I don't think my heart even beats on my way across the room to him.

He meets me halfway.

Complete silence permeates the room. The only sound is the loud thud of my heart.

"She's okay, angel," Tate says as soon as I stop in front of him. "She's okay."

My legs give out beneath me, the weight of the world falling from my shoulders.

Tate catches me before I hit the floor, dragging me into his arms.

I cling to him, sobbing in relief.

CHAPTER NINE

Tate

"Samara," I whisper, brushing strands of hair away from her face. "Wake up, Sleeping Beauty."

"No," she whines, her bottom lip poking out. "It's too early, Tate. Make rounds at a normal person hour for once."

I chuckle, running my fingertips down the side of her face. "Scout's already awake, angel."

She cracks one sleepy eye open, her expression rife with suspicion. "Are you just saying that to get me out of bed?"

"Is it working?" I fight a smile.

"Maybe."

"See for yourself." I lean to the left, allowing her to see the crib.

Scout's strapped into her bouncy seat inside, her wide, solemn eyes locked on Samara through the slats of the crib. Ever since we stopped the sedation drugs two days after her surgery, she spends her time watching the world in abject fascination. Samara is her favorite subject of study. Whenever she's near, Scout's eyes are locked on her.

"Hi, baby," Samara croons, instantly coming alive. She sits upright, her face lighting up with happiness. She rises to her feet, stretching her arms over her head. Her shirt lifts, showing a flash of her sun-kissed skin.

My dick throbs, demanding attention we both know he isn't getting. Not today. It's been a little over four weeks since Scout's surgery. There have been highs and lows, good days, and days that worried the fuck out of me. There were days where Samara wouldn't leave her bedside for even a second, too afraid something would happen if she stepped away. Hell, there were days I didn't leave her bedside, worried as fuck something would happen if I did. But Scout...well, nothing stops Scout. She was born with a warrior's spirit as fierce as her mom's and a heart as pure as her aunt's.

She's the strongest little girl I've ever met. I'm so in love with her. My brothers give me all kinds of grief about it. I don't care. Let them. I held this baby's heart in my hands, painstakingly stitching her back together. You're damn right I'm wrapped around her finger. I'd go to war for her, just like I would her aunt.

After four weeks, we're finally going home. I can't wait to get my girls to Silver Spoon Falls. I can't wait to see Scout grow and thrive outside of the hospital. I can't wait to fall asleep with Samara in my arms, our girl right down the hall. There are a million things I can't wait to experience with these two. Mostly though, I can't wait to have them under my roof, where I can keep an eye on them. Samara won't let me stay overnight at the hospital with them unless I'm off duty, so the last four weeks have come with far too many sleepless nights.

I miss the hell out of my girls when they're here and I'm not. They belong with me.

"Good morning, my sweet, sweet girl," Samara croons to Scout, padding toward the crib. She lowers the side rail and then unlatches the straps keeping Scout in her seat.

Scout kicks her tiny feet, cooing softly.

Samara gently lifts her out of the seat and into her arms, cradling her close. Her nose skims along Scout's crown as she inhales deeply, pulling that fresh baby scent into her lungs. She says she loves the way Scout smells because, no matter what she's going through or how many wires or bandages she has, she always smells like a baby.

She's wire-free now. Her bandages are gone too. Scout has blossomed over the last couple of weeks, shedding monitoring equipment piece by piece. We kept her a little longer than strictly necessary to make sure there weren't going to be more setbacks or complications, but she's finally out of the woods.

She's growing before our eyes. Already, she's a whole new baby, rosy-cheeked and filling out. Her tiny legs have rolls now that she's feeding from a bottle instead of the NG tube that ran down her nose. She got rid of it for good two weeks ago.

"Are you hungry?"

"I fed her, angel," I murmur, stepping up behind Samara and wrapping my arm around her waist. I press a kiss to her shoulder and then her temple, loving the way she melts against me, allowing me to hold them. "We wanted to let you sleep for a little while."

She hasn't gotten much of that lately. No one ever does in a hospital.

Jules came and stayed with Scout twice to give us a break. The first night, neither of us slept a wink. Samara cried most of the night. It broke my heart. I know she needed it though, so I held her through it and let her cry herself out. When she finished, we just held each other until the sun came up. The second night, we made love most of the night. I took her again and again, until she was too exhausted to move.

Jules knew exactly what we'd been up to the next morning when Samara walked around Scout's room like she'd been horseback riding. Her adorable blush every time she looked at me kept me from feeling like a complete asshole. So long as she's happy, I'm happy.

"Do you want breakfast?" I ask Samara.

"Mm, maybe just coffee," she says with a sweet sigh of contentment. "Oh, and a muffin." She laughs quietly. "And a banana."

"I'll give you my banana tonight."

"Tate," she groans. "Not in front of Scout!"

"Are you saying you don't want it?"

"Well, no," she says, looking at me over her shoulder like I'm crazy.

I shake my head, chuckling. "Didn't think so." I press my lips to her forehead. "Why don't you get dressed and start packing up? I'll go get your breakfast, and then work on getting Scout released from this joint."

"Okay," she agrees, her eyes bright with happiness. Her gaze drifts from me to Scout. "What do you think, little one? Are you ready to go home?"

Scout coos again.

"Jesus Christ," Cash mutters, glaring at the loaded wagon I wheel toward him. He rakes a hand down his jaw, looking mildly sick. "Do babies really need all this shit?"

"Yep," I lie. "And you're having two."

Fifth snorts behind him but doesn't call me on my bullshit. Samara doesn't know they're here yet. It's a surprise. They all came to give Scout a proper escort home.

"It's a good thing you're rich, brother," Giant says, slapping my pale best friend on the back before taking the wagon from me. "You want this shit in your cage, Hands?" He jerks his chin toward my SUV, indicating what he means.

"Yeah, thanks." Though where he intends to fit it, I don't know. Between my mom and sister, Troian, Gloria, Jules, and the nurses here, the cargo hold of my SUV overflows with everything Scout amassed during her stay here. And that's after we donated everything we couldn't use.

I'm pretty sure my brothers are responsible for their fair share of the stuff we're taking home with us...like the baby sized cut and pint-sized helmet. I'm not even sure where they found one small enough to fit Scout's tiny head. They'll never admit it, but I think they're all wrapped around Scout's fingers. They're warriors at their core. Nothing riles their protective instincts more than an injured woman or child.

God knows, Scout and Samara riled mine. Falling for them was inevitable. Now, I get to spend the rest of my life loving them.

"I'm going to get my girls," I tell Cash.

"We'll be ready, brother," he promises before sticking two fingers in his mouth and blasting a sharp whistle across the parking lot. "Giant, get that shit loaded. Everyone else, get ready to roll out!"

I leave them scrambling and jog back inside to get Scout and Samara. It takes five minutes to get back to Scout's room.

I find Samara standing at the window, staring out at the city. Scout's asleep in her carseat, a blanket tucked around her.

"Are you ready to go, baby?"

Samara turns to face me, a sweet smile lighting her up. "So ready," she whispers.

I hook my arm under Scout's seat, lifting it gently from the floor, and hold my other hand out to Samara. "Then let's get out of here."

She crosses the room to me, her wide hips swaying. Instead of taking my hand, she rises up to her tiptoes, placing her lips against my jaw. "Thank you," she whispers sweetly.

"For what?"

"For being the best thing that ever happened to me," she says. "For being permanent." She tips her head down toward Scout, tears shimmering in her lashes. "For keeping your promise."

"Fuck," I breathe, my chest pulsing with emotion. "I love you, angel."

She smiles at me again, bright enough to rival the sun. "I know."

"Tate," Samara gasps ten minutes later, stopping in shock when she sees my brothers lined up in front of and behind my SUV on their bikes. "What is this?"

"This is Scout's escort home," I say, smiling. "When wounded warriors return home, MCs escort them whenever possible. Our girl may not have fought for our country, but she fought her own battle, regardless. My brothers are giving her the honor she earned."

"Tate." Tears well in her eyes. "That's so sweet."

"She earned it, baby. You both did." I slide my arm around her waist, pulling her up against me. "You did good, angel. Siobhan can rest easy now."

"Don't you dare make me cry today, Tate Grimes," she whispers, tears already slipping down her cheeks.

"Never," I say, pressing my lips to her temple. "My job is to only ever make you happy."

"I love you so damn much."

"Yeah?" I grin at her. "Then let's go home. I'm ready to show you my banana now."

"Tate!" she cries, burying her face in my shoulder.

"I'm kidding. Mostly kidding," I amend when my dick twitches in protest. "I'm ready to get you home so I can get you naked and convince you to marry me, Samara."

She gasps, her head flying back. Her wide golden eyes meet mine.

"You owe me forever. I intend to collect."

"Oh, I do, huh?"

"Mmhmm," I hum. "Isn't that how the fairytale always ends for Sleeping Beauty?"

"Depends," she whispers. "Is there an apple in this one?"

"I already told you, angel," I growl, nipping at her ear. "You're getting a banana. Now get your pretty ass in the SUV."

"Whatever you say, *Doctor* Grimes."

I swat her ass right there on the steps of the hospital, making her squeal with laughter. She breaks free of my arms and runs toward the waiting SUV, her dark hair flowing behind her, her laughter ringing out around us. God, she's perfect.

"Thank you," I say, casting my eyes up to the sky. I'm not sure if Siobhan can hear me...but I hope she does. I hope she knows her baby girl is going to be fine now, and so is her sister. I'll spend the rest of my life making sure of it.

"Let's go home, baby girl," I whisper to Scout, following Samara off the steps of the hospital and into forever.

Epilogue
Samara

Five Years Later

"Daddy!" Scout squeaks, racing across the living room toward Tate. "You're home!"

"Daddy!" Gemma screams, throwing her blocks and running after Scout as fast as her little legs will carry her. Like her adopted big sister, she's tiny. Unlike Scout, our three-year-old more than makes up for it in volume. Scout tends to be on the quiet side. Not Gemma. She's fearless. You hear her coming from a mile away.

"Quiet, Gemma," I remind her. "Your brother is sleeping."

"Sowwie, mommy!"

I just shake my head, smiling. She'll be yelling at the top of her lungs again in five minutes. Her baby brother, Quade, is only three months old. I think she still forgets that he's here most of the time. She got used to him being in my belly.

She hits Tate like a tiny missile, latching onto his right leg like a Koala.

Tate laughs and reaches down to scoop her up and out of harm's way. As soon as she's secured, he kneels, scooping Scout up too. They both throw their arms around his neck as if they haven't seen him in four years. He's only been gone for an hour. He was dropping his mom and dad off at their hotel. They're in town for the week, though Tate won't tell me why.

He's up to something.

Then again, he usually is.

The ridiculous man spoils me and our babies rotten. He is so good to us. Had anyone told me five years ago that this is how my life would turn out, I wouldn't have believed them. I don't think I was capable of believing them then. For most of my life, I didn't know what it meant to be loved by anyone but Siobhan.

Losing her was, hands down, the most devastating loss I've ever suffered. But it also brought me to the greatest blessings in my life. She put her baby in my care and changed my entire future. She brought me to Tate and Silver Spoon Falls. I lost a sister that day. But I gained a family.

I will always miss her. I will always grieve for her. A piece of my heart will always be missing. But for the first time in my life, the rest of it is full. I know what it's like to have a place in the world now, one where I truly fit. Not just with Tate, but with his family, and the MC, and our friends, and our babies. Silver Spoon Falls isn't just the place I landed. It's my home.

"Shouldn't you two be in bed?" Tate asks the girls.

"Mama said we could wait for you, daddy," Scout says.

"Uh-huh," Gemma agrees. "Her did, daddy."

"I did," I confirm. "Which means it's time for bed now, girls."

"No!" Gemma pouts.

"No pouting, sweet girl," Tate says, giving her a stern look.

She immediately stops pouting, giving him big, innocent eyes. I swear, all he has to do is look at her and she instantly behaves. Not so much for me. Tate says it's because I'm a big softie and she can smell weakness like a baby shark, but he's the one who always gives the girls anything they want! All they have to do is bat their lashes at him and he just says yes. His brothers do too!

They were the worst with Scout. They spoiled her rotten when she was a baby. Her little feet never touched the ground when we were at the clubhouse. Scout is hard to spoil though. She's such a sweet little girl. She is so full of love, and wise beyond her years. I couldn't blame them for wanting to hold her all the time when I did too. She was so snuggly! She still is. I love nothing more than when she crawls into my lap and wants me to hold her.

We officially adopted her when she was two. She calls me her mama and Tate her daddy, but she knows Siobhan gave birth to her. We haven't told her everything, but she knows that Siobhan is in heaven and that she's a hero. When she's old enough, we'll tell her everything she wants to know and get her into therapy to help her work through her feelings about what happened. It's going to be a lot for her to process. It would be for anyone.

For now though, we shower her with love every single day and make sure she knows how much Siobhan loved her. On the rare occasion she asks about her real dad, we tell her that he loved her too. It kills us both to have to tell her anything about him, but I don't want to lie to her or make her feel like she isn't allowed to ask about him or miss him or think about him. Regardless of how we feel about him and the horrible things he did, he kept Siobhan locked up instead of killing her because she was pregnant. I have to believe that's because he loved Scout to some extent.

As for the Savages, well, terrible men usually get what they deserve. The Savages did. Thanks to an undercover cop and a rival MC, the Savages fell one by one. Some didn't live to tell the tale. Others landed behind bars where they belong. If they ever see freedom again, most will be too old to enjoy it. It's justice. As much as men like that will ever see.

The important thing is that they'll never hurt anyone else. They'll never come after Scout. And Scout...Scout is thriving. She's a special little girl with a special little heart. One of Tate's close friends is her doctor now. He takes good care of her. So far, everything has been great. Sometime in the next year, she'll undergo another surgery to extend the tube Tate used to construct her second vessel.

I'd be lying if I said I wasn't nervous about it because I am. But I'm not afraid. Our girl is a warrior, and she'll be just fine. With Tate watching over her, how could she not? That man would go to war for her without even batting an eye. I know because he's done it before.

I don't think I really understood just how sick she was back then or just how risky the surgery was. Jules told me long after it was over how close they came to losing her...and how hard Tate fought. She said he wasn't just a surgeon that day. He was a father. He's been a father to Scout every single day since. She idolizes him. Both of the girls do. But he and Scout share a special bond. I know they always will. He's her hero...but I think she might just be his too.

"Will you read to us, daddy?" Scout asks Tate, her hazel eyes wide and hopeful.

"Yeah, baby girl," he says, pressing a kiss to the top of her head. "Go up and brush your teeth. I'll be right up."

"Yay!" Gemma shouts, flinging herself out of his arms.

"No running on the stairs!" I call after her.

"'Kay, mommy!" she yells back.

Scout stops to give me a big hug and then hurries after her.

"Come here," Tate murmurs, rising to his feet to pull me into his arms. He kisses me hard and deep. "I missed you, angel."

"I missed you too," I whisper, snuggling up against his chest. We haven't had much time together since Quade came home. Between his job, three kids, and my job, quality time is hard to come by. I miss him like crazy.

"Go get ready for bed. I have a surprise for you tonight," he says, kissing me again.

"Your banana isn't a surprise, Tate," I say, snorting.

He swats me on the ass, shaking his head. "Go, smartass."

"Bossy." I bite my lip to hide a smile, kind of hoping my surprise is his banana.

"Be quiet before you wake the kids," Tate growls, smacking my ass as he thrusts into me from behind. His balls smack against my pussy hard enough to sting.

"I can't be quiet!" I cry, grabbing fistfuls of the sheets. My nipples drag across the bedding in the most delicious way, driving me higher. With my ass in the air and my chest pressed to the bed, all I can do is take what he gives me. Every powerful thrust sends a bolt of pleasure through me, each one rising in intensity. I feel like I'm going to crack apart.

"Bite the pillow, angel," he orders me. "Don't make me gag you."

My pussy clamps down on him, his threat making me wetter, hotter. I swear, his filthy mouth should come with a warning label. It does things to me that should be illegal. *He* does things to me that should be illegal. After five years, there is nothing this man hasn't done to me, no way he hasn't taken me.

He even paid Finn an ungodly amount of money to create a VR version of one of my games. Only every character looked exactly like him. Four different versions of Tate made love to me at once that night. I'm still not entirely sure which one was real. He was everywhere at once. It was incredible. I couldn't look at Finn for a month straight.

Six weeks later, we found out I was pregnant with Quade. We haven't tried the game again. I'm a little afraid I'll end up pregnant again if we do. With Scout's surgery coming next year, I want to wait before we have another baby. There's no way I can juggle two babies, Gemma, and Scout's heart surgery.

"Fuck," Tate growls, gripping my hips in his hands and yanking me back onto him. "I love the way I look disappearing into that juicy cunt, Samara."

"Tate," I whine.

"What do you want, baby?"

"More," I demand.

"Greedy girl," he chuckles. His hands tighten on my hips, yanking them up higher. The change in angle is exactly what I need, but that's not enough for Tate. Oh no. He gives me everything he has, driving his hips into me until I'm biting the pillow, trying to cover my screams of ecstasy.

My orgasm rips through me like a bomb blast, detonating again and then again. I'm locked in place, pinned exactly where Tate wants me. He pounds into me, groaning about how good I feel coming all over him. How tight I am. He says the filthiest things as he comes with me.

And then the sweetest.

"God, angel," he groans, falling forward. His head lands against my back. "Every day, I find a new reason to fall in love with you. Five years, and the list keeps growing."

"Tate," I whisper, melting into the bed beneath him.

"You're my world, you know that?" He presses his lips to my back. "I love you, Samara Grimes."

"I love you too."

He stays where he is for a moment and then reluctantly rolls to the side. We both groan when he slips out of me. I hate that part. When he's inside me, I'm complete.

He hooks his arm around my waist, rolling me onto my side. He plasters himself to my back, wrapping himself around me. His face nuzzles into the crook of my neck, his lips touching my shoulder. "You can't go to sleep yet, baby," he murmurs.

"I like you better when you're being sweet to me."

He laughs quietly. "I am being sweet to you."

"Not if you're not letting me sleep."

"You can't go to sleep because you have to pack, angel."

I frown. "For what?"

"We're leaving in the morning," he says, smiling against my shoulder.

"For what?"

"A trip."

"Tate."

His smile grows. "We're going to Angel's island for a few days," he says. "Just you and me. Mom and dad are going to stay with the kids."

I flip around to face him. His dark emerald eyes are soft, his smile wide. "Seriously?"

"Mmhmm." He taps my nose and then tucks pieces of hair behind my ear. "Everything is planned. All you have to do is throw your shit in a bag." His brows furrow. "On second thought, don't pack anything. I plan to keep you naked and on my cock for the next three days anyway. You won't need clothes for that."

"Oh, goodie," I whisper, perfectly fine with this plan.

"You like that, huh?"

"Mmhmm," I hum, snuggling into his arms again. "It means I get to go to sleep now."

He throws his head back, laughing loudly. "You really know how to stroke a man's ego, don't you, Sleeping Beauty?"

"It doesn't need stroking, Tate. It's big enough already."

"That's not the only thing that's big about me, angel. So is my c–"

"–erebellum?"

I squeal with laughter when he flips me over onto my back, coming down over me. His eyes meet mine, full of wicked intent. He pries my legs apart, fitting his body between them. My core clenches, heating for him.

"No sleeping for you," he growls.

"Yay for me," I breathe, chasing his mouth with my own. I'd give up sleep in a heartbeat for another minute with this incredible man. No, that's not true. For him and our kids, I'd give up everything, down to my soul.

Author's Note

If you enjoyed The Surgeon, please consider leaving a review! I appreciate them so much!

Are you ready to take a wild ride with the Silver Spoon MC series? The next book in the series, The Cowboy by Loni Ree, is now available!

Next up from me is Crash into You, a steamy full-length instalove romance featuring an alpha cop and an unwitting murder suspect!

SILVER SPOON MC

These wealthy Texans have it all—Money, looks, power, their MC, and brothers. The only thing missing is someone to share it all with. There's a shortage of eligible ladies in town but these determined men won't let that slow them down. These MC brothers are going to turn the town of Silver Spoon Falls, Texas, on its ear looking for their curvy soulmates.

Beginning in February 2022, Nichole Rose and Loni Ree are bringing you the Silver Spoon MC Series and these aren't your typical MC romance stories. Nichole and Loni like to keep things light. Come along with us on this wild instalove ride.

The CEO by Loni Ree - February 4, 2022
http://mybook.to/TheCEOLoniRee
The Surgeon by Nichole Rose - March 1, 2022
http://mybook.to/TheSurgeon

The Cowboy by Loni Ree - April 4, 2022 -
https://books2read.com/TheCowboyLoniRee
The Heir by Nichole Rose - May 3, 2022 -
http://mybook.to/TheHeirNR
The Rockstar by Loni Ree - June 10, 2022
https://books2read.com/TheRockstar
The Lawyer by Nichole Rose - July 5, 2022
http://mybook.to/TheLawyerNR
The Architect by Loni Ree- August 5, 2022
books2read.com/TheArchitectLoniRee
The Prodigy by Nichole Rose- September 6, 2022
http://mybook.to/TheProdigyNR
The Prince by Loni Ree - October 7, 2022
https://books2read.com/ThePrinceLoniRee
The Bodyguard by Nichole Rose- November 1, 2022
http://mybook.to/TheBodyguardNR

INSTALOVE BOOK CLUB

The Instalove Book Club is now in session!

Get the inside scoop from your favorite instalove authors, meet new authors to love, and snag freebies and bonus content from featured authors every month. The Instalove Book Club newsletter goes out once per week!

Join now to get your hands on bonus scenes and brand-new, exclusive content from our first six featured authors.

Join the Club: http://instaloveinstalovebookclub.com

THE HEIR

Can a billionaire biker and his rival's curvy little sister find forever together...or is blood really thicker than water?

Andreas Romano

Thanks to my father's shady business practices, my life has devolved into putting out one fire after another.

The latest? Dealing with the rival MC he hired to strong-arm federal regulators into looking the other way.

The Hell's Vipers have been nothing but trouble.

Until I stumble across Catriona Grady, their VPs curvy little sister.

Her bright eyes and sweet smile are pure sunshine.

But falling for her promises nothing but trouble for me and my MC.

I guess it's a good thing I've never been one to run from a fight.

Because this little light is mine.

Catriona Grady

People always say blood is thicker than water, but they forget the rest of that saying.

My older brother may have raised me, but he's been nothing but trouble.

He treats me like property, and I'm not interested in being owned.

Until I run into his enemy, Andreas Romano.

When Andreas touches me, I come undone.

I'm falling hard for the gorgeous billionaire.

But there's no way my brother will let him have me without a fight.

It's time to choose my side.

Family...or forever?

NOW AVAILABLE!

CRASH INTO YOU

This curvy teacher never anticipated being charged with murder...or falling for the bossy detective in charge of the case.

Ivy Kendall

Cameron Lewis is the man of my dreams.
Bossy, gorgeous, and fiercely intelligent.
When he touches me, I go up in flames.
There's only one problem.
He's a homicide detective.
And I'm the primary suspect in a murder I didn't commit.
I could lose everything, and so could Cam.
But whoever is trying to ruin my life doesn't get to destroy his too. I won't allow it.

One way or another, I will stop them from harming the man I love.

Even if it means sacrificing myself.

<u>Cameron Lewis</u>
Ivy Kendall thinks she's a fierce tiger.

I know she's a harmless little kitten.

She's also quickly becoming the center of my world.

But nothing is ever simple.

Someone is trying to frame her for a crime she didn't commit.

The closer we get to the truth, the more complex it grows.

Clearing her name will free her.

But learning the truth may destroy her.

I can't let that happen.

I'll protect her, no matter the cost.

Crash Into You is an extra steamy full-length romance featuring a homicide detective and a curvy kindergarten teacher. If you enjoy sassy heroines, OTT protective men, and steamy mysteries, you'll love this gripping romance from Nichole Rose and Ayden K. Morgen!

Crash Into You is now available .

Follow Nichole

Sign-up for Nichole's mailing list at http://authorn
icholerose.com/newsletter to stay up to date on all
new releases and for exclusive ARC giveaways from
Nichole Rose.
  Want to connect with Nichole and other readers?
Join Nichole Rose's Book Beauties on Facebook!

facebook.com/AuthorNicholeRose/

instagram.com/AuthorNicholeRose

twitter.com/AuthNicholeRose

bookbub.com/authors/nichole-rose

tiktok.com/@authornicholerose

More by Nichole Rose

Her Alpha Series
Her Alpha Daddy Next Door
Her Alpha Boss Undercover
Her Alpha's Secret Baby
Her Alpha Protector
Her Date with an Alpha
Her Alpha: The Complete Series

Her Bride Series
His Future Bride
His Stolen Bride
His Secret Bride
His Curvy Bride
His Captive Bride
His Blushing Bride
His Bride: The Complete Series

Claimed Series
Possessing Liberty
Teaching Rowan
Claiming Caroline

Kissing Kennedy
Claimed: The Complete Series

Love on the Clock Series
Adore You
Hold You
Keep You
Protect You
Love on the Clock: The Complete Series

The Billionaires' Club
The Billionaire's Big Bold Weakness
The Billionaire's Big Bold Wish
The Billionaire's Big Bold Woman
The Billionaire's Big Bold Wonder

Playing for Keeps
Cutie Pie
Ice Breaker
Ice Prince
Ice Giant (coming soon)

The Second Generation
A Blushing Bride for Christmas

Love Bites
Come Undone
Dripping Pearls

Silver Spoon MC
The Surgeon
The Heir
The Lawyer
The Prodigy
The Bodyguard

Echoes of Forever
His Christmas Miracle
Taken by the Hitman
Wicked Saint

The Ruined Trilogy
Physical Science
Wrecked

Destination Romance
Romancing the Cowboy
Beach House Beauty

Standalone Titles
A Touch of Summer
Black Velvet
His Secret Obsession
Dirty Boy
Naughty Little Elf
Devil's Deceit
A Bride for the Beast (writing with Fern Fraser)

<u>Easy on Me</u>
Easy Ride
Easy Surrender

<u>One Night with You</u>
Falling Hard
Model Behavior
Learning Curve
Angel Kisses

<u>writing with Loni Ree as Loni Nichole</u>
Dillon's Heart
Razor's Flame
Ryker's Reward (coming soon)
Zane's Rebel (coming soon)

About Nichole Rose

Nichole Rose is a short romance author on the west coast. Her books feature headstrong, sassy women and the alpha males who consume them. From grumpy detectives to country boys with attitude to instalove and over-the-top declarations, nothing is off-limits.

Nichole is sure to have a steamy, sweet story just right for everyone. She fully believes the world is ugly enough without trying to fit falling in love into a one-size-fits-all box. When not writing, Nichole enjoys fine wine, cute shoes, and everything super-natural. She is happily married to the love of her life and is a proud mama to the world's most ridiculous fur-babies.

You can learn more about Nichole and her books at authornicholerose.com.

f

facebook.com/AuthorNicholeRose/

instagram.com/AuthorNicholeRose

twitter.com/AuthNicholeRose

bookbub.com/authors/nichole-rose

tiktok.com/@authornicholerose